Dedicated to my friend Jean Styles. A classy lady.

PROLOGUE

Since the time of the conquistador there had been a legend in the barren lands that fringed the unmarked border. The legend of a merciless horseman clad entirely in grey who appeared from the stifling heat haze of the desert and killed anyone who stood in his way. A creature more akin to a ghost than a living being, the rider had become folklore in the hearts and souls of all those who lived their lives in the harsh landscape which, some said, had been created by the Devil himself. Were the stories true? Had there once been a cruel avenger who had simply killed people for the simple reason that he could? Were the stories based upon an actual man who had lived once upon a time, before history had been recorded? Or, like so many other tall tales, had they been created in the fertile imaginations of simple people who saw demons in every shadow?

All the tales agreed on one thing: the description

of the creature. He was said to be a pale-skinned man with hair the colour of fresh snow. An albino devoid of any hint that there was blood flowing through his veins.

For more than fifty years the chilling stories of the brutal rider had grown more horrific with each telling, lent credence partly by there having been no sign of him during all those decades. Like so many other beliefs in the remotest regions of the West, the stories of the strange creature who destroyed all living things had become little more than myths.

Fables with which to frighten unruly children.

As with all fables, there was an element of truth in the tales, a memory that still haunted the minds of those old enough to recall such a merciless rider in their midst. To those simple people the devilish rider had been real back then, and no amount of mockery could ever make them believe otherwise.

The unforgettable image of that ruthless creature was branded into their very souls. Only death would wipe it away from their memories.

For nearly half a century the pale-skinned creature had slept somewhere off in the barren reaches of the blazing desert. But, as with all sleeping things, there came a time when the creature awoke and began its atrocities once more. Like wildfire, the stories of the creature's return swept across the borderland.

During a season of uncharacteristic twisting storms that crossed the southern deserts one after another until it seemed as though there would never be an end to the destruction they wreaked, a strange horseman appeared, riding a tall grey stallion.

Just as in the legendary stories, this bearded man was devoid of colour in either his flesh or his long white hair. Appearing more dead than alive he had returned and resumed his slaughter.

Staring through small spectacles made of gold and black glass the rider had made his way away out of the treacherous desert and then on from one settlement to another leaving death in his wake.

Once again the stories erupted like volcanos along the border telling of the strange ghostlike horseman who followed the route of the violent twisters. What nature had spared would be shown no mercy by the horseman.

The horseman who feared no living man.

The horseman known as the Phantom had returned.

ONE

The sky appeared to be aflame as the gaunt rider silently steered his tall grey stallion from out of the shimmering desert heat haze towards the small, busy settlement. The day had ended and for many of those who dwelled in Blake's Ridge their lives would soon end as well. A myriad stars started to sparkle across the vast expanse of desert sky as the glowing red-hot-poker heavens faded into black velvet. Amber lamplight cascaded from store fronts and windows as the citizens of Blake's Ridge prepared for the long night ahead. The sound of a tinny piano drifted along the main street from the solitary saloon that stood halfway along the broad thoroughfare. Everything was as it had always been in the hearts and souls of the townsfolk. Nothing was different from all the nights that had preceded it, or so they thought.

Had any of them owned a crystal ball they would have known that this night was to be totally different from all of its long-forgotten cousins. For death was riding into their little tranquil town and death had a way of upsetting things a tad.

The ghostly rider did not move a muscle as the tall grey paced on towards the town as it bid farewell to another day and rejoiced in the arrival of another night. Only the index finger of his left hand teased the reins gently as his mount entered the outskirts of the town. If death had a look then this man had it carved into every inch of his being. His long linen trail coat hung over the cantle of his saddle and two gleaming gun grips hung in holsters to either side of him. He wore no hat, but displayed a mane of long white hair resting on his wide shoulders.

The grey stallion kept on walking. No one noticed its arrival as it bore its hideous master. They were like the desert breeze: totally invisible.

If anyone had taken the time to study the deadly horseman they would have been struck by the black glass spectacles that masked his eyes, the long white beard that covered his shirt front.

Whoever this creature was who sat astride the powerful horse he was nothing like the usual drifter who arrived in Blake's Ridge.

This man was different.

The sound of spurs rang out from his faded sun-bleached boots as he tapped them into the flesh of

11

his horse and turned the stallion towards the noisy saloon. There were two horses already tethered to the hitching pole placed before a trough, but there was plenty of room for more.

Few ghosts could have looked quite as fearsome as the rider as he reined the stallion to a slower gait and approached the rail. There seemed to be no hint of life in the rider's appearance. Nothing but colourless emptiness which even the lantern light could not animate. He drew rein and stopped the tall horse in front of the long hitching rail and simply sat staring over the swing doors into the brightly lit saloon. The sound of the piano playing continued as the people inside the room went about their business, unaware that they were being observed.

A few cowboys staggered out of the Bucking Bronco but their eyes were blurred by the effects of bellies full of whiskey. The horseman watched them as they made their way along the boardwalk, then turned his neck and looked around the wide street. A few of the stores were still open for business, but many more were already locked up tight.

The horseman tilted his head back as he heard the sound of females and their clients above hint in the rooms behind a veranda that ran the length of the building. Open windows allowed lamplight to spill out across the thoroughfare, along with the usual noises with which he was familiar.

12

The rider averted his gaze and lowered his head. It was obvious that the females were busy earning their keep. The rider raised his lean frame up, slowly drew his right boot from its stirrup, then swung his long leg over the saddle cantle.

In one easy movement the rider clad in grey had dismounted and looped his reins over the end of the long hitching pole. Then he secured the leathers with a tight knot. He stepped up on to the boardwalk and looked at the two horses standing next to his own. They were small and stocky mustangs, unlike his own magnificent thoroughbred.

He rested a hand on the nearer of the swing doors and gazed in at the room. Tobacco smoke lingered about five feet off the sawdust-covered floor and the piano player kept hammering the keys of his well-used instrument. The Bucking Bronco was far better kept than most saloons he had encountered. It even had wallpaper and a carpeted staircase. Yet none of this impressed the man who watched the dozens of men and women from behind the black glass of his spectacles.

With an ease which few could ever emulate he entered the saloon silently. He had crossed halfway towards the long bar before the first of the saloon's patrons to notice his arrival in their midst drew the attention of others to his presence among them.

The piano stopped playing.

An uneasy silence filled the saloon.

Every eye watched the haunting figure as he strode towards the bar. The sound of his spurs suddenly became the only noise inside the Bucking Bronco. Half a dozen lamps cast their light upon the strangest creature any of its customers had ever seen before.

There was no colour in his flesh. No colour in his hair. No hint of life to be seen. Only corpses looked the way he looked but this man was walking. Dead folks never walked. The spooky figure was not only walking; he had the tails of his thin duster pushed over his gun grips in readiness like a gunslinger.

The black glass that shielded his eyes chilled and frightened in equal measure as he turned his head from side to side, as though studying those who watched him. The bar girls took refuge behind their potential clients and yet even the broadest-shouldered of the men did not make them feel any safer.

They say that the eyes are the mirror of a man's soul but what of the man who has no soul?

The ghostly apparition reached the counter, then stopped. He looked at the long mirror behind the barkeep and studied the activity behind him. He did not move a muscle.

'What'll it be, stranger?' the bartender asked as he polished a glass with a white napkin.

'Whiskey?'

There was a long pause.

The bartender placed the glass down and leaned

on the counter, trying vainly to see the eyes hidden behind the two circles of black glass.

'Whiskey?' he repeated.

'Nope,' the man replied.

'Then what ya want?'

'Hickok,' the man whispered. 'Is he here?'

The bartender smiled. 'Wild Bill Hickok?'

The colourless man gave a slight nod of his head. 'The same.'

The bartender curled the black-waxed tips of his moustache with the fingers of both hands and shook his head. 'Nope. Ya missed him by a whole day, stranger. He left here about sundown yesterday on the east-bound stage. Had his black roan tied to the tailgate.'

The stranger ran the fingers of his left hand through his mane of white hair. He glared at the smiling bartender before him and inhaled sharply. 'Ya find something amusing, little man?'

The bartender rested his hands on the counter. 'I sure do, stranger. I sure do.'

'What exactly do ya find so amusing?' The voice was rasping, as though the man had swallowed broken glass. 'Tell me. I'm mighty interested.'

'You. I find ya mighty sorrowful and that's a fact.' The bartender laughed and pointed at the tall creature who stood before him. 'Just look at ya. Are we meant to be feared of some old varmint who ain't had the guts to go to a barber for about twenty years or more?'

As though fuelled by the courage of the man behind the counter the rest of those inside the saloon started to laugh out loud as well. Soon the Bucking Bronco was filled with the sound of men and women laughing.

The ghostlike man said nothing.

He did not have to.

His hands would do his talking for him.

Faster than any of the laughing people had ever seen anyone's hands move, the stranger slapped leather. His hands had drawn, cocked and fired quicker than the blink of an eye.

Two bullets hit the bartender in the chest. Plumes of gore splattered over the mirror and trailed down its surface. Then the gaunt figure swung on his heels with his smoking weaponry in his pale hands. Yells and screams came from all directions. A well-dressed man tried to reach the swing doors but a bullet caught him in the back of his neck. He crashed on to a table, sending cards flying into the air. A cowboy rose with a bar girl still on his lap and drew his gun. Before his thumb had clawed back on its hammer two more shots hit him and the bar girl. Blood sprayed up the wall behind them before they fell lifeless to the floor.

The laughter had turned into screams.

Deafening screams.

Hysterical screams.

16

Another bar girl ran for the rear door but she was also cut down by a lethal shot. It went through her bare back and sent her falling into the sawdust.

One by one the bullets hit every single one of those in the large saloon room as the demonic gunman paced around firing his guns. Droplets of blood hung in the air as though caught by the tobacco and gun smoke as the last of them were slain.

Within a mere minute every one of the men and women who had surrounded the ghostly killer were lying dead or dying.

The man with the mane of white hair walked towards the staircase. He could hear muffled, fearful voices coming from the rooms on the landing. By the time his right boot had been placed on the bottom step he had reloaded both his weapons.

With trails of smoke billowing from the barrels of each gun the killer slowly started up the staircase.

The sound of his spurs played a deathly tune.

TWO

Even after the deafening sound of the shooting had faded into the fabric of the bloodstained saloon walls the acrid stench of gunsmoke still lingered inside the Bucking Bronco. Like ghostly whispers the smoke slowly drifted out of the bullet-ridden saloon into the street, where a crowd of terrified people hid within the shadows, watching and waiting for a glimpse of the gunman.

There was only one sound remaining inside the Bucking Bronco and that was the macabre melody of the spurs worn by the man who had brutally killed everyone within the saloon.

A thousand eyes watched the saloon.

No one could comprehend what had occurred. They had all been drawn, like moths to a naked flame, to the saloon when the shooting had erupted inside it. Yet even after more than half an hour the curious still did not have the courage to venture anywhere close to the now baleful building.

Inside, blood trailed down the once pristine walls and gathered in congealing pools. On the sawdust-covered floor a number of bodies lay amid the gore. A few of the saloon's oil lamps had managed to survive the bullets that had spewed from the barrels of the blazing guns as the brief onslaught had raged.

Dead men and women were also lying on the stairs leading up to the small well-used rooms on the second storey. No one had survived the murderous attack.

No one but the strange albino drifter.

At first sight it might have seemed that the carnage had been random but in truth this had been a well-rehearsed slaughter.

Those who lay dead would never know why they had been chosen for destruction. That was only known to their killer.

There had been no mercy shown by the victor of this outrage as he had massacred all those who had been unfortunate enough to find themselves staring down the barrels of his guns. No one had managed to stop him once he had started. No one had even managed to wound him as they had fired their guns in feeble response.

The sound of spurs rang out again as the killer checked that none of his victims remained alive.

A shocked concerted gasp from the shadows sounded along the dark street as the onlookers caught a brief glimpse of the unholy apparition moving in front of the flickering oil lamp in one of the rooms behind the veranda.

A heartbeat later and he was gone from view.

The spurs jangled as the colourless figure stepped out on to the landing and made his way to the top of the long staircase. He paused and stared down into the large room at his barbaric handiwork before shaking the spent casings from his guns and reloading them in turn.

Not one of the people out in the shadows had dared to venture closer than a street's width towards the saloon since the shooting had started. Even the long delay since the final shot had not given them renewed courage. They all knew that whoever it was who had been dealing out death inside the Bucking Bronco was still there.

Still ready and willing to kill again.

The shadows of the street were filled with men, women and even children. They watched the silent building as people often fearfully watch things they cannot understand. It was not the building itself they feared but the unknown creature who was still inside its four walls. The creature whom they had just seen in one of the windows.

Whispers swept across the town from shadow to shadow as people created monsters with their

20

imagination and tried to guess what sort of person could walk into a saloon and simply turn it into a slaughterhouse.

Surely no *man* could do such a thing?

It had to be something far worse than a man.

Courage had never been in abundance in the small town known as Blake's Ridge. People here had never had any call to be brave, for they had hired the best sheriff money could buy to be courageous on their behalf. But tonight the sheriff was not in town and the townsfolk had been virtually stripped clean of anything but terror. Although most of the men in Blake's Ridge had guns hanging from their hips few if any knew how to use them. Holstered guns were like fashion items. They looked good but only a handful of those who wore them knew how to use them. Even fewer could have fired their weapon in anger to wound or kill another living being.

The whispers grew more urgent. The speculation as to what sort of monster was inside the saloon became more monstrous. More ridiculous. More fearsome.

The gunman on the saloon landing could hear the frightened voices of those outside in the street. It did not trouble him one bit as he dropped one smoking gun into its holster and firmly gripped its reloaded twin.

Slowly he began to descend the staircase into the

main room of the Bucking Bronco. His spurs rang out a hollow heart-stopping tune as they caught the rucked carpet which was now stained with fresh blood. He lifted a boot and carefully stepped over a corpse left riddled with his bullets halfway down the stairs. No hint of emotion showed on the face of the albino assassin, who kept one of his guns clutched firmly in his hand.

The merciless killer walked through the haze of gunsmoke towards the long bar. The congealing blood was sticky and clung to his boots but he ignored it. Broken glass from dozens of shattered whiskey glasses covered the top of the wet counter. The aroma of whiskey filled the nostrils of the man as he kicked aside the body of a bar girl and stepped behind the counter to where a score of glass bottles remained intact amid the broken ones beneath the long mirror.

He snatched one of the bottles off the shelf. Ignoring the sticky blood of the bartender which covered its surface and label he raised it to his lips. He gripped the cork with his teeth, eased it free of the bottle's neck, then spat it away. His eyes never stopped darting all around the room from behind the black glass of his spectacles as they searched for something else to kill. He studied the carnage before him with a satisfied smirk. Every body was unique. Each twisted in its own special way, according with the way death had come to it.

Five of the bodies were female, yet the man who gulped on the hard liquor had killed them with equal viciousness.

They had been dispatched to their Maker, just as had their male counterparts. He showed no living creature any clemency, whatever its gender.

The whiskey bottle did not take long to empty.

Killing was thirsty work.

The man rubbed his beard along the back of his sleeve and then carefully placed the empty bottle down on the shelf. The mirror was splattered with lumps of flesh, which had been blasted out from the back of the bartender when two lethal bullets had driven into him. The ghostly creature picked up a bloody nugget of flesh and swiftly wrote on the mirror. A message written in blood to chill those who would read it after his departure. When satisfied with his scribbling he tossed the hideous lump of flesh aside, stepped over the dead bartender and out into the heart of the silent saloon.

He kept his drawn gun aimed at the swing doors as he slowly made his way through the bodies on the crimson-coloured sawdust.

Each victim was checked to ensure there was no hint of life remaining in any of them. Even the slightest trace of life would have brought another bullet hurtling into their heads. But as he made his way towards the swing doors and the dark street beyond there was no sign of any life in any of them.

They were exactly what they appeared to be.

They were dead.

As the tall figure reached the swing doors he plucked a hat off the floor, placed it on his head and pulled its brim down to ensure it stayed on his white hair. Its previous owner's blood trailed down his mane of long white hair but either he did not notice or he simply did not give a damn.

His left hand pushed the swing doors apart and he walked out on to the boardwalk. There was a cool breeze but he did not give it a second thought. Hey had other interests and they were glaring out into the darkness from the shadows all around him. He knew they were there watching him. They were always there in every town he had ever visited.

The shadow people.

He released his grip on the swing doors behind him and listened to them rock on their hinges. He stepped out under the porch lantern and allowed its almost orange light to illuminate his horrific features. A gasp went around the shadows like a wildfire.

They had seen him.

He spat at them in contempt.

Their whispers intensified as they focused on his tall lean form and tried to convince themselves that this was a man, not a monster whom they were looking at.

Yet no man had ever seemed quite so unholy or frightening.

Even the hat could not hide the white hair which hung over the collar of his coat on to his wide shoulders. His bearded face was hidden by shadows and not one of the most curious of the townspeople wanted to get any closer to try and see what he really looked like.

The man reached down and tugged the reins to his grey stallion free of the hitching rail. He then looked at the two mustangs which stood beside his own impressive mount.

He cocked his gun hammer and levelled the weapon at them.

To the total shock of the onlookers he fired twice. Both mustangs fell on to the sand as fountains of blood curled up from their shattered skulls.

Again the grim figure spat.

The killer stepped into his stirrup and threw his leg over his saddle. He gathered the reins, then swung the grey around and held it in check for a few moments as he studied the shadows as an eagle studies its prey.

Not a word was spoken.

He drove his spurs into the flesh of the grey stallion. The animal responded and thundered down the long street with its master standing in his stirrups. Every eye watched the rider who had the still smoking gun clutched in his right hand. He whipped the shoulders of the powerful animal beneath him with his long rein tails. Dust rose up into the air from beneath the horse's hoofs.

Before it had time to settle the weird horseman had disappeared from sight. Devoured by the blackness of night.

A crowd of people rushed to the saloon from the protection of the shadows.

Some went inside.

Most remained on the boardwalk and fearfully peered into the Bucking Bronco. The sight of all the dead bodies made them gasp in horror.

Then another gasp went through the crowd as they all seemed to see what was written on the bar room mirror at the end of the long room at exactly the same moment.

Words written in the blood of those who lay dead inside the saloon chilled every one of them to the bone.

Two words were emblazoned upon the mirror.

Every voice seemed to say the pair of words in unison.

'The Phantom.'

'Can't be,' a frail voice piped up as an ancient, crippled man hobbled through the crowd and entered the Bucking Bronco. 'It just ain't possible.'

'What in tarnation are ya talking about, Silas?' one of the younger men asked the bow-legged Silas Barker as his eyes squinted at the red words on the mirror. 'That's what it says. Whoever that bastard was, he calls himself the Phantom.'

The old man's weathered left hand held on to the back of a hardback chair as he eased his old bones down upon it. 'But it just can't be him. Can't be him.'

The crowd concentrated on the terrified face of the man who kept staring at the mirror.

'Can't be who?' another of the people asked.

'The Phantom.' Silas sighed. 'Last time I seen him was when I was barely out of my teens. But he looked exactly the same back then as he does now. Skin and hair the colour of bleached bones and eyes hiding behind black glass.'

'Ya memory is playing tricks with ya, old-timer.'

Silas shook his head. 'Listen up. Ya don't forget a critter who puts two bullets through ya leg bones and leaves ya crippled, boy. That was him OK, but how? No man can live that long without time either killing 'im off or leaving 'im like me.'

'I heard them stories about the Phantom,' a voice said from the back of the crowd. 'Nothing but a mess of tall tales. This varmint is just using the legend to spook us all.'

'Listen up.' The old-timer buried his face in his hands and started to sob like a scolded child. 'Forty or fifty years back he come out of the desert and started killing. Killing just like this. He kept on killing for months and then disappeared. Everyone figured he must have bin killed himself but others said ya can't kill a ghost. A phantom just can't be killed. After all these years he comes back and starts all over again. I know it ain't possible but look around here. It's the same mindless slaughter like the last time. No reason for it but here it is all the same.'

'Ya saying this ain't a real man that done this, Silas?' a trembling voice asked the old man. 'Ya saying this is the same critter as in all them old stories?'

'Fruit of the Devil's loins.' Silas sighed. 'That's what they called him last time he was on the rampage. Ya got a better way of explaining this?'

One of the womenfolk rested a comforting hand on the bony shoulder. 'I don't understand, Silas. Who is this Phantom? Has he got a real name?'

'Old or not, Silas, this gotta be the work of a real man,' one of the younger men said with a snarl. 'There ain't no such beast as a ghost or the like. Whoever done this was real and alive.'

Silas swallowed hard. Tears filled his eyes as they studied the carnage before them and he recalled the name he had not heard for more than half his life.

'Axil Gunn. That was it. Axil Gunn,' the elderly man muttered fearfully. 'Leastways, that was what some folks reckoned his name was, but he favoured being called the Phantom.'

Every eye returned to the words written on the mirror as the blood trailed down from each crude letter.

THREE

The noon stage from Rio Hondo was on schedule as it carved a route down through the moonlit terrain towards the way station at Apache Springs. The six horse team were spent as the driver drew back on the hefty reins and slowly brought the stagecoach to a grinding halt inside the walls of the Overland Stagecoach Company's most southern way station. A score of lanterns swung in the evening breeze, casting their light upon the dust-caked vehicle as its guard dropped down to the ground and beat his hat against his pants leg. Dust floated up into the black sky as three burly stablemen came rushing out from the adobe building.

Luke Peters, the driver, let out a long breath and kept his boot firmly pressed down on the brake rod until he had wrapped the reins around it. His wrinkled eyes watched the stablemen set about their duties. Each knew what his own task entailed and they went about unhitching the team from the traces and leading the steaming animals away towards the livery stables set against a high white-washed wall.

'And don't ya go bringing a fresh team until me and Clem have had our vittles, ya hear?' the driver yelled out at the three men as they led the six exhausted horses through the corral. 'I ain't gonna be rushed tonight. I needs me my rest.'

None of the men responded or even acknowl-edged the rantings of the old man. They had heard the exact same words a hundred or more times.

Rance Howard had been the manager of the station for three years and always thought he had once been destined for something better. Now he accepted his lot, as most men of a certain age tend to do. Holding a tin cup filled with coffee in the palms of his hands he ambled out of the main build-ing and stood bathed in the amber illumination. He raised his coffee cup as if in salute to the driver, then smiled at the guard who staggered wearily towards him.

'When's the company gonna hire a good driver, Rance?' Clem Carter asked, vainly trying to rub the pain from his buttocks. 'That old fool could hit a pothole even if it was up on the moon.'

'Ya looks mighty tuckered, Clem,' Howard remarked to the guard. 'Have any trouble?'

The guard paused and replaced his hat on his head. 'No trouble exceptin' for them damn holes on the trail. One day some smart varmint will flatten that trail out so I don't have to have my bones loosened up every time we drives across it.'

Howard sipped at his beverage. 'Luke's OK. He's just a tad hard of seeing.'

Clem turned to the driver. 'Hear that, Luke? Rance says ya blind.'

'Shut the hell up, Clem.' The driver chuckled. 'I'll buy ya a fancy little cushion to sit on when we gets to Cactus Flats.'

'See what I'm up against, Rance?' the guard complained.

Howard patted the man's arm. 'Easy. He's harmless.'

Clem watched as the manager eased his boot leather closer to the lip of the boardwalk and squinted into the dark interior of the carriage.

'Ya got a passenger?'

'Sure have.' The guard grinned. 'We sure had us a bit of fun back at Rio Hondo, Rance.'

'A real special passenger and no mistake.' The driver leaned over from his lofty perch and started to climb carefully down to the ground. 'Got us an unexpected passenger back there. He was intending on staying there to play himself some cards but the sheriff had other ideas and kicked him out.'

Howard looked interested. 'Who got himself kicked out of Rio Hondo, Luke? What he do?'

Clem sighed. 'He didn't do nothing except get off in Rio Hondo. That was enough for the sheriff back there.'

The station manager took another sip of his black brew. 'I don't understand. Why'd this critter get himself ejected from Rio Hondo if'n he never done nothing?'

Luke Peters gave out a belly laugh. 'Some folks have themselves a reputation that kinda rides ahead of them.'

'What?' Howard lowered his cup.

The driver winked and then opened the carriage door. 'We're here, Mr Hickok. Apache Springs way station.'

The station manager looked at the guard and gulped. 'Wild Bill Hickok?'

'Yep.' The guard nodded. 'The one and only.'

From the darkness of the carriage interior the tall figure of one of the West's most notorious sons emerged. His long brown hair hung on his elegant coat shoulders as he straightened up his tall frame and studied the way station before him with his famed hooded eyes.

'Greetings, Mr Hickok.' Howard said.

Hickok gave a slow nod, then turned his head and looked down at the wrinkled old-timer who was still holding on to the door handle.

'I was asked politely to leave Rio Hondo.' Hickok corrected the driver. 'Nobody kicks Wild Bill out of any town.'

The driver started to chuckle. 'I ain't gonna argue with ya, Wild Bill. I likes living too much.'

'You are smarter than you look, driver.' Hickok pulled a silver dollar from his pocket and slid it into Luke Peters' grubby right hand.

'Thank ya kindly.' The driver chuckled.

Then Hickok noticed the open-mouthed expression on the face of the station manager. 'Can one of your boys see to my black roan back there, friend? He needs water and grain.'

Before Howard had a chance to answer the driver pocketed his silver dollar and slammed the carriage door shut. 'I'll look after that beauty myself, Wild Bill. It'll be a darn honour.'

The driver rushed to the tailgate where he released the reins of the tall stallion and led it towards the stables. Hickok stepped up on to the boardwalk, which stretched the full length of the building. He paused and looked Howard in the face. 'You the manager of this station, *amigo*?'

Howard nodded shyly. 'Sure am.'

'I'll want a room, grub and a bottle or two of whiskey.' Hickok said. He placed his flat-crowned Stetson on his head and peered into the brightly lit interior. 'I was intending to stay back at Rio Hondo for a while, to play some stud but, as you heard, I have had to change my plans. Folks sure ain't very friendly in these parts. I had me the same trouble back at Blake's Ridge a couple of days back. Do you have any vacant rooms?'

Howard nodded again. 'Sure do. We got us six rooms for passengers and every one of them is empty.'

'I'm expecting a couple of friends to catch up with me at any time. We were meant to meet at Rio Hondo but as you'll have figured out already, I'm not there.' Hickok drew in breath and seemed to grow in height. 'I'm sure that my friends will follow when they learn what happened.'

The station manager just kept staring at Hickok, his head gently nodding.

Hickok noticed the strange expression on the manager's face and leaned closer. 'Something troubling ya?'

The station manager lowered his cup from his mouth and looked at the famous face before him. A face he had seen on a score of dime-novel covers. Howard could barely believe that Wild Bill looked exactly as he did in all of the dime-novels' illustrations. The only difference was that Hickok was far taller than he had ever imagined.

'You *are* Wild Bill Hickok, ain't ya? The *real* Wild Bill Hickok I done read about?' Howard nervously stammered.

'Yep.' Hickok answered from behind the drooping

moustache which hid his lips. 'Ya heard of me?'

'Sure have.' Howard thrust out a hand. 'May I shake ya hand, Mr Hickok? May I have the honour? My name's Howard. Rance Howard.'

'I sure hope ya vittles are as obliging as your manners, Mr Howard.' The famous visitor accepted the handshake and then entered the well-lit main room followed by the manager and shotgun guard. He gracefully made his way towards the roaring fire that burned in a stone fireplace.

Howard grabbed the stagecoach guard by the shoulder and leaned over. 'That's the genuine Wild Bill Hickok, Clem.'

'So?'

'I done read books about him,' the manager gushed as he watched the every movement of the man warming his hands. 'I never thought I'd ever meet him though. Hell, he's famous.'

'He's also trouble,' Clem whispered quietly. 'Mighty big trouble.'

A bewildered expression filled the manager's face. 'How can ya say something like that?'

Clem smiled. 'I can say it coz it's darn true, Rance.'

The guard moved to a long table and sat down just as a well-built female of about forty summers emerged from the kitchen carrying a massive black coffee pot. Howard finished his beverage and walked to where the woman had placed the large pot. He rubbed his neck and refilled his cup. He could not shake the words of the stagecoach guard from his mind. To him Hickok was a legend. A hero. He believed every word he had read about the famous man who somehow seemed to be from another time. A time when the West was truly wild and men like him tamed it.

'What's on the menu?' Hickok asked as he turned away from the warmth of the fire and looked at the manager. 'I'm hungry and got me a thirst. Bin eating dust for the longest while.'

'Stew,' Howard answered. 'Stew and biscuits.'

Hickok frowned. 'Reckon that'll have to do.'

'We got us a plentiful supply of whiskey though.' Howard waved an arm in the direction of the bar set to the side wall of the entrance to the kitchen.

Hickok glanced across at the bar. A smile hid behind his drooping moustache. The array of whiskey bottles drew him across the well-brushed sod floor until he reached the counter.

'Ya got a mighty fine selection of whiskey here,' he said. His long fingers searched one of his pockets for a coin.

'Ya thirsty, Mr Hickok?' Howard asked. He followed the tall man who was now resting the palm of his left hand on the polished wooden surface of the counter.

'I'm Wild Bill, Mr Howard.' Hickok slammed down a fifty-dollar golden eagle, turned a whiskey glass over and pushed it forward. 'I was born thirsty. Pull a cork and start pouring.'

Rance Howard dutifully obeyed.

FOUR

A swirling cloud of choking dust rose up above the prairie floor and hung above the thundering horsemen as they forged on through the moonlit sagebrush towards the line of high mesas and the next settlement. To unsuspecting eyes they appeared like a troop of ghosts. Ghosts hunting in a pack. Each of the fifteen riders was caked in a hundred miles of dust as they crossed the arid terrain and then continued on towards the distant border town of Blake's Ridge.

Although weighed down by pounds of trail grime none of the intrepid horsemen had any desire to stop and clean up. They were on a mission. A mission to catch up with a deadly maniac who had already left scores of innocent people dead behind him in half a dozen other remote towns.

A hundred miles of hard riding had brought them from the prosperous city of Badwater to a place more suited to the Devil than creatures with real blood flowing through their veins. They valiantly spurred on through the hostile landscape knowing that it was their duty to try and stop the killer before he struck again.

It sounded easy enough.

Too easy.

The truth was far harder to swallow. Although they had managed to close the distance between themselves and their prey, he was still ahead of them. Ahead of them and still killing as he headed further and further into the unforgiving territory.

So far the line of horsemen had never managed to get within half a day of the elusive escaped maniac whom they had been ordered to destroy. Most men who managed the near impossible and escaped from Badwater's notorious lunatic asylum were swiftly captured and returned.

But not this one.

There was something very different about this escaped asylum inmate. He might have been branded as insane but he had proved to be the rangers' most elusive and cunning of foes.

The fifteen riders had soon realized that this evasive customer was far from the jibbering idiot that they had at first thought him to be. He had managed to steal a horse, guns and enough provisions to last a month within hours of breaking out of the secure madhouse.

Escape had not been enough to satisfy his depraved cravings. He had wanted revenge. Revenge for what they had done to him over the decades during which he had been imprisoned. After escaping he had simply murdered his way across the sprawling city and continued killing as he rode deeper into the place of his creation. Even before he had escaped the towering walls of the asylum he had taken out his merciless fury upon its doctors and staff.

Twenty years of brooding and planning had made it easy.

None of the horsemen knew the true identity of the creature they trailed. In all of the decades during which he had been chained up like the creature he was he had never spoken a single word.

Some had thought he was a mute.

Even when he had been subjected to the most torturous of treatments designed to cure him, his spirit had not been broken. He had silently endured everything they had subjected him to and never allowed them to crack the cast-iron resolve with which all maniacs protect themselves.

They would all pay. Pay the ultimate price for the indignities they had showered upon him. He had spent over twenty years plotting revenge. The pale-skinned man had dealt out his own brand of justice to all those who had dared to keep him chained up like an animal.

41

Badwater asylum had tasted his own personal brand of revenge.

A chilling tally of five bodies lay slaughtered within the high walls of the asylum before the murderous albino had even reached the city's streets. A couple of decades of legal torture had resulted in a fearsome man becoming ten times more lethal and insane.

If there had ever been a spark of humanity inside him it had surely been destroyed by those who thought they were saving or curing him.

A hundred miles of dry wasteland lay behind the riders as they drove their mounts on into the night. Every dozen or so miles they had come across a new village or town. None of them had managed to escape the deadly fury of the creature the rangers sought.

In each of those towns the two same words had been left painted in blood, proclaiming that the man they sought was called the Phantom.

It was as though the years of being jailed inside the large asylum had built up a volcanic rage so devastating that now it could do nothing but erupt and envelop the innocents who had the misfortune of lining the route he had chosen.

The leader of the horsemen was Captain Bodie Jones. He had lived his entire adult life serving in the Texas Rangers. He was a man who followed orders and never once questioned those whom he considered his betters. But even Jones had never seen anything like the carnage he and his men were discovering at regular intervals along the arid trail. The seasoned officer had started to think that they were not chasing a man at all but something only using the guise of being a man.

A wolf in sheep's clothing.

Each of his followers was cut from the same cloth as Jones himself. Like their leader they were seasoned rangers who did as they were told, yet even they had become wary of what or whom they were pursuing.

The line of horsemen kept going as they had done during the long ride from Badwater. Each of the riders knew that this was one man they could not afford to let slip from their grasp. At all costs he had to be caught and killed as soon as possible. There were already half a dozen towns behind them littered with the bodies of those who had fallen prey to the deadly pale-skinned butcher.

The rangers spurred on.

They knew that the murderous albino rode and slaughtered during the hours of darkness and then somehow vanished as soon as the sun rose. Night after night he had appeared and killed and then disappeared.

The mountainous mesas offered a million hiding-places along their endless walls of ancient rock. As the night neared its last couple of hours the rangers drove on hard, following the trail that they knew their adversary must have taken since his last outrage. They all knew that somewhere above them he might already have decided to rest for another day. Creatures without any hue in their skin hid from the blistering rays of day.

Caked in the dust of a hundred miles of relentless pursuit the fifteen rangers again saw another small town ahead of their snorting horses. Each of them in his soul knew what they would soon find there. It would be exactly the same pattern as all those blood-soaked towns left in the wake of their horses' hoof-dust.

Another mindless slaughter.

The town ahead of them was quiet. There were no tinny out-of-tune pianos playing or sounds of the normal revelry common along the border such as the rangers expected. The town was deathly silent and the horsemen knew why. They steered their mounts past the wooden marker which proclaimed the name and population of the small settlement and rode into its wide main street.

'Brush them stars clean, boys,' Jones ordered his men as he rubbed a sleeve cuff across his Texas Ranger star. 'We don't want no bullets coming our way. Let them know the rangers are in town.'

Captain Bodie Jones rode into Blake's Ridge's main street ahead of his men. Then he saw the crowd still gathered outside the Bucking Bronco. As the rangers drew their reins and stopped beneath the saloon's façade they realized that once again they had arrived too late.

Jones dismounted and pushed his way through the crowd to the swing doors and stared inside the saloon. His eyes narrowed as he looked at the mirror with its crude writing. He swallowed hard.

The Phantom had struck again.

FIVE

An entire day had come and gone. A tad short of twenty miles from the carnage at Blake's Ridge the slightly larger settlement of Rio Hondo stood amid a landscape of tall grass and a plentiful supply of fresh creek water. Usually it was a place where people spent the hours of darkness enjoying what little they had to the sounds of laughter and the smell of tobacco smoke, but not this night.

This night their peace had been shattered into a million fragments. Those who had survived were left huddling together in the darkest of shadows. To the eyes of approaching drifters there seemed to be nothing wrong. Nothing except the scent of the gunsmoke that floated on the cold night air.

A canopy of black velvet stretched across the heavens from horizon to distant horizon. Thousands of diamonds sparkled around a bright moon in the frosty night air. There was not a cloud to be seen anywhere above the high grass range which spilled out in all directions from beneath the hoofs of the two thundering horses as their masters spurred them on. The rising hills that flanked the small settlement stood black upon a high ridge. Set half a dozen miles behind the array of brick and wooden buildings that made up Rio Hondo rose a wall of rock, and above it towered cliffs and mesas. Beyond that was the beginning of the desert. A blistering desert, where the lone albino horseman took refuge as soon as the sun rose to announce the start of a new day.

Dust floated up into the crisp night air off the hoofs of the two horses as their masters guided them to the tree-covered ridge. From this elevated vantage point there seemed to be nothing untoward down on the range or in the town of Rio Hondo.

Nothing except an eerie silence.

That and a familiar fragrance well known to all those who lived their lives carrying a gun.

The scent lingered on the evening air as the two horsemen crossed the moonlit stream and drew rein on the very top of the high ridge. Steam floated from both riders and their exhausted mounts and ascended to the canopy of branches and broad leaves.

The riders inhaled and dwelled upon the scent which drifted from the town below them. They recognized the tang of gunsmoke.

Yet there was still no noise.

No sound of guns or rifles being discharged by drunken men as they enjoyed themselves. There was nothing but silence. Not even the calls of night birds on the wing greeted their ears. It was as though the world had died and nobody had bothered to tell the two saddle-weary riders.

Neither horseman said a word as their horses' hoof-dust continued on down the steep slope towards the town below their resting place. The town below them was of average size, yet there was hardly a light burning anywhere along its main street. The moon cast its unearthly illumination across the town and danced across the stream that ran from the ridge down to the edge of the small town.

Both horsemen were tired, but one of them had realized as soon as they had drawn rein that something was not right. Something just did not add up.

Veteran gunfighter Tom Dix eased himself off his high-shouldered gelding and dropped the reins to the ground. He crouched and kept squinting down to where the town seemed to be sleeping far below them.

His partner dismounted slowly, placed a hand against the pit of his spine and leaned back until he heard the familiar clicking of his ancient bones. Dan Shaw was a retired lawman and had seen most things in his fifty-some years but knew that there was plenty yet to discover. He sighed, dragged his canteen from the horn of his saddle and unscrewed its stopper.

'Why'd we stop, Dixie?' Dan asked, and took a long swig of the stale liquid. 'Damn. We're so close to Rio Hondo we could spit and hit the place. Why'd we drag leather?'

Dixie did not look up at his friend. His eyes kept burning through the moonlit air down to where the town stood. He pulled out a silver timepiece and flicked its lid open. The moon lit up its enamel dial.

'I make it about ten, Dan,' Dix said drily and snapped the lid shut again.

Shaw nodded. 'Sounds about right. Not that it makes any difference what the damn time is. Dark is dark in my book.'

Dix stood and pocketed the watch. His eyes remained glued on the town as he stepped to where the older man stood. 'Don't it seem a bit odd to ya, Dan? That town is mostly unlit. Folks don't go to bed this early in these parts. Don't that make ya kinda wonder?'

The ex-marshal turned thoughtfully and stared down to the moonlit buildings. He rubbed his jaw.

'Damn. I never thought about that,' Dan agreed. He sniffed the air. 'There ain't hardly a light down there. A few at the very edge but the middle is totally dark. I can smell gunsmoke as well.'

'Yeah.' Dix nodded. 'An awful lot of gunsmoke if my nose ain't lying to me. That much smoke don't come from the gun of a liquored-up cowpoke. I figure some serious shooting took place a short time back.'

Dan scratched his neck. 'Yeah. Rio Hondo is usually lit up for the fourth of July every night of the week. This don't make no sense. No sense at all.'

'And the last time we was here I recall there being over ten saloons on Main Street alone. They don't shut for business 'til the roosters wake up. How come their lights ain't blazing, Dan? How come?'

'That's right, Dixie.' Dan stepped back to the stream and lowered his canteen down into the fresh fast-flowing water. 'It sure is strange for a town like Rio Hondo to be shuttered down like that. What do you reckon is going on down there?'

'Something awful bad,' Dix answered as his partner lifted the canteen up from the stream and screwed its stopper back on. 'Towns like Rio Hondo don't ever sleep. They also don't stink of gunsmoke. A few miles back I thought I heard me some thunder but now I'm figuring that it was gunplay I heard.'

'Yeah, there was a bunch of sounds like thunder about ten minutes back,' Dan agreed. 'Must have bin shooting.'

Dix sighed deeply. 'But who was fanning their hammers and why, old friend? That's the question.'

Dan hung his canteen back on his saddle horn and ran a hand down the neck of the tall animal. It was well lathered up after the long ride they had undertaken.

'Our horses are tuckered,' Dan observed. 'We'll have to bed them down for the night when we hits town.'

Dix did not respond to his partner's statement. He kept staring at Rio Hondo with anxious eyes. 'What's going on down there?'

'Nothing.' Dan shrugged. 'Listen. Ain't a sound. If there was shooting going on it must have ended a while back.'

'Ended?' Dix raised an eyebrow. 'Ended or just paused?'

Dan grabbed the mane of his mount.

'Ya figure old Wild Bill might have done something down there, Dixie?' Dan asked. He lifted a leg and stepped into his stirrup. 'Our old pal can be a little troublesome. What if he was shooting up the town and they all hightailed it for cover?'

Like a man half his age Dix threw himself on to his tall horse, poked the other boot in its stirrup and gathered in his reins. 'Even Wild Bill wouldn't put a whole town on the run, Dan. Nope. Something else has happened down there by my reckoning.'

'Something pretty damn bad.' Dan eased his horse around until he was facing his friend. 'You got the same burning in ya craw that's eating at my innards, Dixie?'

'Yep.' Tom Dix gave a firm nod and swung the gelding around to face the apparently sleeping town below them. 'Sure have, pal. My innards are plumb aching. I want me some answers.'

Dan Shaw pulled the brim of his hat down. 'Reckon we ain't gonna find us no answers up here, Dixie. Ya ready?'

'Damn right I'm ready.'

Both horsemen let out a yell and spurred. Both the sweating horses started down the steep slope at breakneck speed. Dust rose into the night sky above the riders as they urged their mounts on.

Within seconds they had reached the flat range and were thundering across its swaying dry grass towards the still silent Rio Hondo. The gathering frost which tipped every blade of the tall grass was burst apart as the two horses ploughed a course directly towards the settlement.

The air appeared to be filled with a million droplets of ice but neither rider noticed as they forged on. Their full attention was on the line of buildings which was getting closer with every stride of their mounts' long legs.

Dix rose in his stirrups and balanced above the neck of his horse. He glanced at his friend. He was about to call out when suddenly the sound of guns being blasted rang out and vibrated over them.

Whatever had occurred in Rio Hondo was happening again.

Both determined horsemen narrowed their eyes and looked straight ahead. More deafening shots echoed off the weathered structures from somewhere among the maze of streets. Flashes of deadly light lit up the darkness ahead of them.

Dan pressed his boots into his stirrups and leaned as far back as he could. His horse almost fell as it skidded to an abrupt stop beneath him. Dix pulled his own leathers up to his chin and the gelding dug its hoofs into the ground. Both men looked at one another in surprise.

The shooting rang out again.

'Must be a mighty big fight by the sound of it, Dixie.'

Dix swung his mount around and brought it to trot to the side of his partner's horse. 'That ain't no gunfight, pard. That's just one gun hammer being fanned. Listen up.'

'Are ya sure?' Dan cupped an ear with the palm of his right hand.

The expert gunfighter gave a slow nod. 'I'm dead sure. Only one gun was being fired.'

Pitiful muffled cries followed the sound of shooting. They soon faded as death claimed the victim. There was a pause in the gunfire, then more shots rang out from somewhere in the town. Both men could see smoke rise from over the roof shingles like a genie escaping from its bottle.

'The critter reloaded and is now firing two guns

at the same time, Dan.' Dix dragged his reins to his left, screwed up his eyes and stared hard and long at the town ahead of them. Then he could see the tell-tale flashes as bullets erupted from smoking barrels. He raised a hand and pointed. 'There. Do ya see it, Dan?'

Dan was confused as he steadied his skittish mount. 'I ain't sure of nothing, Dixie.'

The shooting stopped again.

Swiftly Dix flicked the leather safety loops from the hammers of his matched pair of holstered Colts. 'He's reloading again. C'mon, pard. Now's our chance to ride in and see who is shooting the town up.'

Before Dan could say a word Dix had spurred and was galloping towards Rio Hondo like a man possessed. The retired lawman whipped his long leathers across the back of his mount and followed his friend.

'Wait up, Dixie,' he called out vainly.

Tom Dix did not slow his pace.

Both riders thundered on towards the town.

A dozen gaps between tall moonlit buildings offered them many choices of a way into the heart of the dark town but Dix chose the direct route. Dix drew one of his guns, cocked its hammer and steered his tall horse straight at where he could see the flashes of gunplay.

The sound of his horse's hoofs reverberated off

the sides of the two buildings between which he was navigating. Then his eyes narrowed as venomous tapers of deadly gunshots sped like quicksilver before him in the street. With each shot the main street lit up for a brief heartbeat.

Dix knew it only took one of those bullets to put paid to even the toughest of souls. With gritted teeth the gunfighter drew rein just as his horse cleared the two buildings and emerged into the street, between two troughs and hitching rails. The gelding obeyed its master and abruptly stopped. There were dead bodies strewn everywhere around the main thoroughfare. They lay beneath the illumination of countless stars and an unforgiving moon. The smell of fresh gunsmoke filled Dix's nostrils as he fought with the powerful gelding. Then he felt the heat of a bullet as it passed within inches of his face a split second before the deafening noise of the shot reached his ears. The bullet had come close to finding its target. Too damn close for the gunfighter's liking. Instinctively Dix raised his gun and fired into the cloud of gunsmoke as a chunk of wood from a porch upright just behind him shook with the impact of his attacker's bullet. Splinters burst from the dry wooden upright and showered over both horse and rider. Defiantly Dix swung his mount around. The seasoned gunfighter tried to see the man with the smoking guns but all he could make out was a silhouette as it advanced and fired again.

Dix ducked just as a bullet tore his battered old Stetson from his head. Like a man diving into a pool Dix threw himself from his horse and crashed onto the ground. The gelding reared up and kicked out at the air as its master hid in the shadows of its long legs and tried to find a target.

Dix was just about to fire when Dan emerged from between the two buildings atop his sweating buckskin. The retired lawman stared down at his friend open-mouthed.

'Get down, ya old fool.' Dix yelled out at his partner. 'Ya a sitting target.'

Dan felt the bullets pass all around him. 'I see him, Dixie.'

'He's seen you as well, ya old locobean.' Dix grabbed hold of his partner's sleeve and forcefully yanked him off his saddle before more shots came seeking them out. The retired lawman hit the ground hard and growled as he clawed at his gun and drew it.

'Who is it?' the winded Dan groaned.

'How the hell do I know who he is? Whoever it is he's shooting at us.' Dix crouched and vainly tried to get a bead on their attacker but both their horses were bucking erratically, making it impossible to aim at anything.

Dan managed to roll over as the hoofs of his own horse came crashing down on to the ground next to him. 'These nags are mighty scared, Dixie.'

56

'They ain't as scared as I am.' Dix spat as he rocked back and forth trying to find a gap between their terrified horses through which to see the man who kept on firing at them.

Dan screwed up his eyes and then gasped at the sight which surrounded them. 'There's bodies all over, Dixie. Folks and horses lying dead all over the place.'

'If I don't kill this critter we'll be joining them,' Dix gritted as another volley of bullets cut up the air around them.

The mysterious rider spurred his tall grey to advance. As the grey stepped forward the gunman reloaded his guns, then trained them on their new targets.

Dix rested a hand on Dan's shoulder and looked under the belly of his horse. Again he tried to fire but the terrified gelding kept obstructing his aim.

Both kneeling men suddenly saw the moonlight dance off the barrels of the guns in the rider's outstretched hands. The rider squeezed the triggers of both guns at exactly the same moment. Plumes of hot lightning flashed from the gun barrels and cut across the distance between them. Then the rider repeated the action. A circle of choking gunsmoke suddenly masked the advancing horseman from view.

Four shots.

Four deadly shots.

Piteous noises came from both their mounts as the horseman's lethal bullets found their targets. Fountains of warm blood spewed over both kneeling men as the horses shuddered as the bullets hit their skulls. Death rippled through the hefty animals. The gelding fell first, nearly crushing both Dix and Dan as it hit the ground. The buckskin took a little longer to succumb to the fatal impact. It bucked and then turned before dropping like a felled tree. With a fountain of red gore rising from the hole in its skull the stricken creature shuddered on the ground.

More shots rang out. Dix and Dan threw themselves up behind the side of their prostrate horses as the horseman's lead buried itself into the flesh of the dead animals.

'Kill him, Dixie,' Dan pleaded as the choking gunsmoke grew more intense. 'Kill him before he kills us.'

Without any hint of fear Dix leapt to his feet. He stood and started to fan his gun hammer feverishly into the swirling smoke left by their attacker's guns. But to Dix's utter surprise the rider did not return fire.

Then Dix heard the sound of hoofs echoing as the rider cut up through a side street and headed for the open range.

Dan scrambled back to his feet. 'Did ya get him, Dixie? Did ya kill the bastard?'

Dix remained silent as he stared into the cloud of dust and smoke that filled the gap between the two buildings. Slowly the smoke drifted away. Both men stared around the street in disbelief. Neither had ever seen so much death in one place before. It chilled them.

They then looked at one another and shook their heads in mutual bewilderment.

'Where'd he go, Dixie?' Dan asked as he staggered away from his fallen mount. He screwed up his wrinkled eyes and darted his gaze from one shadow to the next. 'He disappeared.'

The seasoned gunfighter walked round the dead horses and looked down between two buildings at the range beyond. He could just make out a cloud of dust rising as the sound of hoofs faded away. He raised his gun and aimed it between the buildings. 'He lit out thataway, pard.'

'Shoot,' Dan urged.

'He's out of range, friend.' Dix rubbed the grime from his face along his sleeve and spat at the ground again as he stared at their dead mounts.

Dan Shaw looked all around the main street and saw that every horse within its length was lying where it had been slaughtered. He gave out a long sigh and looked at his partner. Dix seemed to be stunned as he shook the spent casings from his gun.

'Both our horses are done for, Dixie boy,' Dan

said. 'Looks like most of the other nags in town are also now nothing more than potential gluepots.'

Dix gave a slow nod and started to pull fresh bullets from his belt to reload his weaponry. 'Yeah. I figured that.'

Dan moved to his friend. Dix was pale. Even the eerie light of the moon could not disguise the fact that something had chilled the gunfighter to his very soul.

'What's wrong, Dixie? Ya looks like ya just seen a ghost, friend,' he remarked.

Tom Dix tilted his head and looked at Dan.

'I reckon I just did see me a ghost.'

'What?'

Dix dropped the gun into its holster and tightened his gloves over his knuckles. He turned away and stared down at their dead horses.

Dan Shaw grabbed hold of his partner's shoulder. Their eyes met.

'What ya say, Dixie?'

'I said I seen me a ghost,' Dix repeated.

People started to emerge from the shadows all around them and hesitatingly moved towards them. Dix inhaled deeply.

'Didn't you see his face, Dan?' Dix asked. 'When he opened up with his hoglegs the flashes lit up his face. Didn't ya see his face?'

Dan Shaw shook his head. 'All I seen was the flashes of his guns, Dix. I closed my eyes and was praying that ya might get a clean shot at him before he sent us packing to our Maker.'

Dix bit his lip. 'I saw his face. Just for a second as he fired his guns. I sure caught sight of his face.'

'And?' Dan shook his partner's arm.

'I once saw that hideous face before. Twenty or more years ago I come close to having my head blown clean off by that critter,' Dix recalled. 'I tell ya, Dan. It ain't the kinda face ya ever forget, pard. I'll never forget that face as long as I live.'

Dan searched for his tobacco pouch. 'Who the hell was it, Dixie? Spit it out.'

'A critter I thought was long dead.'

'Yeah, but who was it?' Dan urged. 'It sure weren't no ghost that killed our nags. Ghosts kinda shy away from using guns, I'm told. They cotton to scaring folks to death, not putting lead in them.'

Tom Dix swallowed hard but there was no spittle to lubricate his dry throat. He rested his hands on his gun grips and tilted his head until he was looking straight at his friend.

'It was Axil Gunn, Dan.'

Dan gulped. 'The Phantom?'

Tom Dix gave a slow nod.

'Yep. The Phantom.'

SIX

It was early. The fiery sun had barely risen above the bloodstained town of Rio Hondo as the two determined men marched the length of the main street and barged their way into the sheriff's office. It had been barely an hour since the fearsome outrage but both men still could smell the gunsmoke in their flared nostrils and taste the bitter flavour of revenge in their dry mouths. In all of their days neither had ever felt so angry before. It showed in every line on their seasoned faces.

The door of the office rattled on its hinges as the dust-caked and bloodied pair strode towards the seated man behind the cluttered desk. As always Dix led the way as they approached the ashen-faced lawman who sat staring at a mug of cold coffee as if it might provide his confused mind with the answers he craved.

Sheriff Hal Tyler had barely heard his door open

but his tired eyes looked up at the two men who cast their shadows across his ink blotter. He was a broken man. A man whose entire life and reputation had been destroyed by the brutal assault on his once peaceful town. His courage had been tested and it had failed him as it had failed so many other men who had set eyes upon the killer known as the Phantom.

He remained silent.

Dix rested the knuckles of his gloved left hand on the desk and leaned over. His eyes burned into those of the bewildered lawman. He slammed his fist down and shook the very fabric of the building.

'Well?' Dix snarled at the man he and his partner had known for nearly ten years, a man he no longer recognized.

Tyler remained quiet.

'Was ya asleep when all this killing took place, Hal?' Dix shouted furiously. 'Was ya?'

The sheriff remained quiet.

Dan took hold of Dix's arm and gently pulled him back. He recognized a man in shock and Tyler was deeply drowning in his own broken thoughts. He moved closer to the stunned lawman wearing the tin star on his shirt front and rested a hip on the edge of the desk. Tyler's attention drifted to the retired marshal.

'Are ya OK?' Dan asked.

Sheriff Tyler looked as though he had been

kicked by a herd of mules. There was a sickness in his heart. He had known every one of the victims who had fallen prey to the mysterious killer known as the Phantom. He grieved for them all and for his own pitiful lack of courage when faced down by a creature hell-bent on killing.

'What's the matter with him, Dan?' Dix probed.

'Easy, Dixie,' Dan said in a soft tone. 'This man is hurting real deep. He ain't gotten a grip on what's happened.'

Dix fumed. 'He's yella.'

'Maybe. Maybe not.' Dan sighed. 'Some folks just ain't got the vinegar when it comes to facing folks like Gunn. You were once the highest-paid hired gun in the south but even you couldn't get a bead on that critter, Dixie. What chance would a man like old Hal have against the likes of him?'

'I guess ya right.' Dix turned and paced around the office as his eyes kept staring out at the dead bodies now being bathed in the morning sun.

Tyler reached for his mug, then changed his mind. His fingers fell short of the handle. He leaned back on his chair and glanced at the ceiling of his office. He drew a deep, noisy breath and looked back at Dan. There were tears in his eyes.

Dan leaned over until his face was less than a foot away from that of the shaking lawman.

'It was the Phantom that done this, Sheriff,' Dan said. 'Axil Gunn done this. Nothing ya could have

64

done to stop him. Even Dixie here couldn't best him out there.'

Tyler blinked hard. 'I . . . I heard of him,' Tyler managed to say. His hands started to shake as though an earthquake was erupting inside him. 'But I thought Gunn was dead. Dead a whole lifetime ago.'

Dix was frustrated. He was not used to seeing grown men broken the way Tyler was broken. He moved to the door and stared out at the carnage still cluttering the street. He gave out a long angry sigh.

'Don't go fretting none, Sheriff,' Dan said, patting the seated man on the shoulder. 'The Phantom is a locobean. No man can ever tell what someone like that is gonna do.'

Tyler looked Dan in the face. 'I heard the shooting. It started slow at first and then kinda grew. I heard folks screaming out there but when I caught sight of him on that tall grey I was just too scared to show my face. I never seen anything that looked like that in all of my grown days.'

Dan looked at Dix, then returned his attention to the sobbing man. 'Must have bin a whole heap of shooting to leave as much death as that.'

Tyler nodded and rubbed his face with the tails of his bandanna. 'That's right, Dan. It was as though a war was going on out there. A war to end all wars. A war waged by just one man. If'n he was a man. I reckon Rio Hondo played host to the Devil himself last night. He was killing like I never seen no one kill before. I went to the door but then I seen him. I never seen anyone look like that before. He was like something concocted in ya worst nightmares. I never even managed to open that door.'

'Ya yella,' Dix snarled.

Tyler nodded. 'I'm yella all right, Dixie. Ya right. I'm still alive though. I'd not have lasted any longer than all those dead 'uns out there if I'd tried to stop him. Nothing could have stopped him. He weren't like regular folks, I tell ya. It was the Devil and no man can fight the Devil.'

Dan waved a hand at Dix, then drew Tyler's attention once more. 'Don't go blaming yourself, Sheriff. Ya right. No regular man can fight a maniac.'

'Ya could have damn well tried.' Dix spat. 'Ya might have saved some of them folks out there if ya had just tried, Hal. One lucky shot might have slowed the bastard up a tad.'

Tyler buried his face in his hands and started to sob like a child. 'Don't ya think I don't know that, Dixie? I might have saved some poor critter from being killed but I just froze. I never seen anyone that looked the way he looked. I've faced down a few gunslingers in my day but that critter was like a gun-toting ghost. No colour in his face at all. His eyes hidden behind them black glass spectacles. His long white hair and beard down to his buckle. His guns never quitting. Axil Gunn ought to be dead long ago and maybe he is and that was some avenging ghost we all done seen.'

Dan stood back up and licked his dry lips. He knew only too well what it was like being a lawman out of your depth. When does a coward become no more than a fool? Take on too much and just end up being buried in boot hill?

Dix glanced back at the sheriff and shook his head sadly. 'I still reckon ya should have tried, Hal.'

'Easy, Dixie. Hal here ain't no gunfighter. He don't know how to handle his hogleg the way you do. Hell. I could never hit the side of a barn unless I had me a scattergun.'

Dixie marched back to the sheriff. 'Listen up, Hal. Me and old Dan here needs us a couple of fast horses to replace the ones Gunn killed an hour or so back if'n we're gonna have us a chance of catching that critter. Do ya know of any nags still left alive in this town?'

Tyler gave a confident nod. 'Rufus Garrod got himself a whole string of fine horses just south of town in a small draw. He breeds them and makes himself a pretty penny.'

There was a long silence. Dix bit his lip. 'How far south of town is his spread, Hal?'

'No more than two miles,' the sheriff answered.

Dan and Dix looked at one another. Both men knew that they were not as spry as they had once been. A two-mile trek was something neither of them favoured.

'Are there any nags left in Rio Hondo ya might be able to get someone to ride to Rufus's ranch?' Dix asked.

For the first time for hours the sheriff rose to his full height and walked to the door. He dragged his hat off its stand and opened the door. He felt the heat of the new day greet him as he forced himself out on to the boardwalk. Dan and Dix trailed him silently as Tyler flagged down a youngster who looked little more than ten or twelve. The boy had been studying the dead horses still tethered to hitching rails along the main street. When he saw the sheriff waving to him he ran to the weathered lawman and smiled.

'What ya want, Sheriff?'

'Listen up, Johnny,' Tyler began. 'Is ya pa OK?'

'He sure is, Sheriff. We stayed in the livery behind the hay bales in the loft until that crazy galoot finished his killing and rode out.'

Tyler looked at the men standing behind him. 'Johnny's pa runs the livery.'

Both men nodded to the still smiling child. He nodded back.

The sheriff returned his eyes to the boy. 'Are there any horses left in the livery, Johnny?'

'A few.'

'Could ya borrow one and head on out to Rufus's place and buy a couple of horses for my friends?'

The smile on the boy's face grew wider. 'I sure could. If'n ya give me the money, that is.'

Tom Dix stepped forward until he was shoulder to shoulder with the sheriff. He pushed his fingers into his pants pocket and pulled out two golden eagles. They glinted in the morning sun as he handed them to the boy.

'Reckon this'll be enough, Johnny?' Dix asked.

The boy gasped as he looked at the two coins in the palm of his small hand. He slowly nodded and looked up into the gunfighter's eyes. 'Are ya gonna catch that varmint that killed all these people and horses, mister?'

'Yep,' Dix replied confidently. 'Catch and kill him, son.'

The boy looked excited. He turned and ran down the street to where the livery stable stood.

'I'll get ya the best two horses Rufus has got,' he called back over his small shoulder.

Dan stared grimly at two men in the street. Two men clad in black tail coats who were busily gathering up bodies and stacking them up on the back of a flatbed wagon. A few others were trying to work out what to do with all the dead horses that the Phantom had left in his wake.

'How long do ya figure it'll take little Johnny to

get back here with the horses, Hal?' Dan asked the sheriff.

'Half an hour or so,' the sheriff answered.

Dix raised a leg and placed his boot on a trough. He sighed and spat. 'I reckon the reason Gunn killed all these horses was to stop him being followed.'

Tyler waved a hand at the bodies. 'But why kill all these innocent folks? They never done him no harm.'

'The Phantom always was loco.' Dix shrugged. 'If we knew the answers to why he done this I reckon we'd be loco as well.'

A man with his arm in a sling ambled in and out of the sunlight along the boardwalk towards the three men. He was covered in blood but most of it was not his own. He reached them and paused.

'Doc,' Tyler acknowledged. 'Looks like the Phantom got you as well.'

Doc Smithers concentrated on the weary lawman. 'I was in the Bucking Bronco when that madman come bursting in last night, Sheriff. I managed to hightail it out through the rear when he started shooting but not before he winged me.'

Tyler inhaled deeply. 'Leastways ya survived. That's what counts. Rio Hondo couldn't exist without you.'

'I thought ya might want to know what that bastard asked the barkeep before he began his killing,' Doc Smithers offered.

All three looked at him.

'What he ask the barkeep, Doc?' Tyler wondered.

'He asked Riley and then the crowd where Hickok was.' Smithers sighed. 'Someone told him that Hickok had been kicked out of town. The crowd started joshing him and he got real angry. Then he started shooting.'

The men watched as the injured doctor made his way back towards his small office. Tyler rubbed the sweat from his brow.

'This is all my fault, boys. My fault.'

'How'd ya figure that, Hal?' Dan asked.

'I kicked Wild Bill out of town.' Tyler muttered. 'I heard tell of his bad ways and didn't want him in Rio Hondo. If I'd let him stay then the Phantom wouldn't have slaughtered all these innocent folks.'

'I'll wager ya wrong, Hal.', Dan sighed.

Dix rested a hand on the sheriff's shoulder. 'I wonder why that maniac was looking for Wild Bill Hickok, Hal?'

The sound of a solitary horse drew all their attention as Johnny Parker rode past the sheriff's office and headed off towards the small horse ranch.

Dix looked at his partner.

'C'mon, Dan. We better get our saddles and gear off them dead horses of ours and wait for that boy to get back here with some fresh horseflesh.'

Tyler watched the two sturdy men as they headed

to where the bodies of their dead animals still lay. He turned and thought about the question Dix had posed.

Why did the Phantom want Hickok?

SEVEN

Sunup had arrived barely an hour earlier but the rising sun was already mercilessly blazing down across the land on either side of the long border. Yet, the streets of Blake's Ridge were not bustling,as they usually were, with people going about their daily rituals. There was a sadness in the town as people tried to come to terms with the unimaginable horrors of the night before. Yet no matter how much the townsfolk pondered on what had happened, none of them could understand the incomprehensible. For no sane mind can ever fathom one that is abnormal. No peaceful person will ever know why some creatures desire only to inflict pain and worse. So it was with the grim-faced folks who strolled aimlessly along the boardwalks. They were lost. Lost to wander in the avenues of confusion until their minds healed again.

Captain Bodie Jones and his men had slept tethered to their horses in the corral beside the livery stable. They had awoken as soon as the sun had risen from beyond the high scarlet-coloured mesas and cast its blinding rays across the small town.

Blake's Ridge was still silent as the sturdy Texas Ranger eventually hoisted himself up from his bedroll and released the reins from around his boot. The tall man knew that once again they had managed to arrive too late to prevent further mindless slaughter. A few hours of sleep had not made him feel any better or rested his confused and angry brain.

Jones cast his eyes around the corral where they had spent another fruitless few hours trying to rest both their bodies and their minds. His men were already awake and ready to start out after their elusive prey once more, but years of experience had left their commander less assured. Seasoned rangers cut from the same mould as Jones knew only too well that sometimes the vermin they hunted could turn the tables on them.

Jones walked between his men and inhaled the aroma of the fresh bacon being fried in the black skillet atop the makeshift fire in the centre of the corral.

'Ya want some vittles, Captain?' a weathered veteran of more than twenty seasons named Toby Hope asked as he tumbled the bacon around in the skillet with a Bowie knife.

For the first time since they had set out from the

distant Badwater Jones waved a hand of refusal. He had no appetite for anything except capturing the killer as soon as possible and stopping his insane progress.

So far all Jones seemed to have done since they had set out after the Phantom was witness countless dead bodies. The slaughter had grown more and more sickening as they had vainly chased their maniacal prey.

Lesser men might have already quit but not these hardened souls. They were rangers and only death stopped rangers.

Captain jones vowed that the killing had to stop and stop fast. Yet how could they stop the Phantom when they could not even manage to get close to the maniac they hunted?

Years of experience meant nothing.

They were being mocked and people kept dying.

'Ya gotta have yaself some grub, Captain,' Hope said as the rest of the men accepted their rations from his well-used skillet. 'Ya can't ride all day without anything in ya guts.'

Jones gave a slow shake of his head. He knew Hope was right but he felt sick at the memory of what had greeted them only a few hours earlier. In each town they had trailed the madman to one opera of death after another.

Murdered victims of both sexes and of all ages had greeted the rangers' arrival each time. It was as if the Phantom knew exactly how close his pursuers were and somehow managed to flee just in time.

'I ain't got me an appetite, Toby,' Jones admitted. He reached down to the campfire and plucked a tin mug filled with strong black coffee. Even the smell of the coffee turned Jones's normally cast-iron innards as he paced to the fence poles. He rested the mug on the top pole and stared out at the still stunned inhabitants of the town. People were not walking purposefully around, as was their usual habit, but simply roaming listlessly. Every noise drew their eyes and chilled their souls. These people were terrified that the ghostly killer might return to continue his brutal killing.

The ancient ranger Toby Hope got to his feet and ambled across the baking sand to where Jones rested against the fence poles. He leaned his thin frame against the weathered wooden poles and looked at his troubled friend.

'Ya looks mighty upset, Bodie. More upset than I ever done seen ya,' Hope said in a low whisper.

Jones flashed an eye at the older man. 'Yep, old-timer. I sure am. This critter we're hunting ain't like anyone else we've had to track.'

'The varmint is plumb loco, Captain,' Hope said. He pulled out his tobacco pouch and started sprinkling the makings on to a gummed paper. 'I bin on this earth a whole lotta years and I ain't never come across anyone like him. He just kinda cottons to killing and that ain't right.'

Captain Jones nodded and blew at the rim of his mug.

'I'm starting to think that we ain't chasing us no real man at all, Toby.' Jones sighed. 'Whatever he is he sure ain't like no other man I ever come across. Even the most crazy of cowpokes I ever encountered weren't as blood happy as this 'un is. Kinda scares me. He kills the way most folks spit.'

Toby Hope's few stained teeth pulled the drawstring tight and allowed the tobacco pouch to hang from one of them. His tongue ran along the gummed paper's edge. 'You scared? I don't believe ya. Bodie Jones ain't never bin scared of nobody in all the years I've known ya.'

'I am now.' Jones sighed. 'Scared of what this man is capable of if we corner him. Ya might not know it but I like you boys and I sure don't want to lose any of ya.'

'The Phantom.' Hope said the name bitterly as he pulled a match from his vest and ignited it with his thumbnail. 'What kinda critter calls himself something like that? And how come? Ya figure he just wants to scare us off? Stop us from hunting his hide?'

Jones managed to take a sip of the black beverage. 'That can't be it. He don't even know we're trailing him, Toby. He ain't trying to scare us off coz he ain't got no idea that we're after him. Nope. He's just killing coz he likes killing. Calling himself the Phantom 'coz there's a legend in these parts of such a creature.'

The older ranger blew a line of grey smoke away. 'Sounds like he's trying to scare folks. Do ya figure madmen want to scare folks?'

Jones shrugged. 'He scares me. Scares me about thinking of what he might do next. Maybe he'll attack a bunch of children next. Who knows what he's capable of?'

Toby Hope ran a hand across his neck as the temperature grew more intense. 'And there ain't never a sign of him when the sun comes up. That's kinda spooky, Bodie. How come he just disappears during the day and how come he's always ahead of us once the sun sets again? How does he do it?'

'If I knew that I'd be able to figure out how we can get the drop on him. Get ahead of him.' Jones riled. 'If he is a man like you and me then he's sure the strangest one we'll ever be chasing. But if he *is* a real living and breathing man we can kill him. Real men die, Toby. Die real easy sometimes.'

'I sure hope we gets him in our sights soon,' Hope said, staring at the smoke rising from the tip of his cigarette. 'I reckon he'll lead us all over Texas otherwise. There could be a thousand dead folks lining the route unless we do manage to kill him pretty soon.'

'We're like hounds chasing a real smart racoon,

Toby.' Jones finished the coffee and handed the mug to his friend. 'Tell the men to eat up and then make sure their horses are fed and watered. Stock up with provisions and fill every canteen. We gotta get him. I don't care if we don't sleep for the next week, Toby. He has to be stopped.'

'Where we headed next?'

The ranger captain tilted his head and pointed towards the edge of Blake's Ridge and the dusty trail. 'Thataway. Rio Hondo.'

'That makes sense. He's not missed out one damn town along the trail since we started following him.' Hope shook the last droplets of the coffee from the tin mug. 'When we starting out?'

'As soon as them horses have bin grained and watered, Toby.'

Hope gave a salute and moved to join the others.

Jones remained resting his elbows on the top fence pole.

EIGHT

The way station at Apache Springs was quiet. Too quiet for the liking of its manager Rance Howard. He knew deep down in his guts that something was wrong. The fiery sun slowly climbed up into the cloudless blue sky, creating dark shadows that spread from the towering mesas and across the sagebrush-littered prairie. Nothing appeared to be alive out beyond the way station's four sturdy adobe walls. Nothing but the haunting whispers of an invisible breeze which moved the sand as it rolled down from the high blood-coloured rocks.

If it were not for the deep well of crystal-clear water set in the middle of the station neither man nor beast could survive in this unholy terrain. Yet for some reason Howard felt there was another creature surviving out there somewhere. It was a foolish thought for a logical man, but Howard could not shake the notion from his weary mind.

Was there someone or something out there watching the station? Apaches perhaps had returned to their ancestral lands and were waiting to strike as they had frequently done years before. Could that be it? Were his instincts warning him or was it just the fact that he was tired?

Howard had been up before dawn, as was his habit. The stagecoach from Rio Hondo had still not arrived to change teams of horses. At first it had not troubled the experienced man but as hour followed hour whilst the relentless morning sun kept rising, Howard had started to become concerned.

It was a long stretch of sand between Rio Hondo and Apache Springs. An awful long way with little or no protection for a stagecoach carrying a strongbox destined for Cactus Flats. It only took one ambitious outlaw or bandit to lie in wait and even the best stagecoach guard had little chance of defending a moving vehicle. Beads of sweat trailed down from the band of his Stetson and followed a route to his already sodden bandanna.

For the umpteenth time Howard tried to reassure himself. It was not unusual for coaches travelling in either direction to be late. A busted wheel or a horse throwing a shoe could pitch the schedule into disarray easily in this rugged terrain. But he had never known any of the stagecoaches to be this late.

He checked his timepiece again. It was nearly noon and that clawed at his innards. If a stage had trouble that they could not fix then it was company policy for either the driver or the guard to use one of the six-horse team to ride to the nearest station and get help. Yet there had been no sign of anyone. Howard walked slowly up the steps until he reached the parapet beside the east gate of the station. He placed both his hands on the whitewashed adobe wall and looked out into the shimmering haze.

Where were they?

His employees were all going about their duties in the stable and the corral. They, like the manager, were totally confused. A fresh team of horses had been ready and waiting to replace the horses from the dawn stage for hours. He watched his crew throwing buckets of water over the harnessed animals in an attempt to keep them calm as they waited in their traces. Howard bit his lip and kept searching the desolate landscape before him. It stretched for as far as the eye could see. A desert of sand and cactus, sage and salt-brush, the sand bleached of all its colour. Only the Joshua trees resembled anything remotely lifelike. He wanted to see dust rising up into the sky. Dust kicked up by the hoofs of a six-horse team. There was nothing.

'Ya looks a tad troubled there, Howard.'

Howard swung around and looked at the familiar features of the man known as Wild Bill Hickok as he slowly ascended the mud-brick steps to the highest point in the station.

A slim cigar poked out from the dark drooping moustache of the famous man as he reached the parapet and stopped. Smoke trailed from its tip as the hooded eyes stared out at the land that surrounded them on all sides.

'What's eating at ya, son?' Hickok asked. 'I noticed ya pacing like a caged cougar for hours.'

'The dawn stage didn't show, Wild Bill,' Howard answered drily as he turned to face the hostile scene before them once more.

'That unusual?' Hickok removed the cigar from his mouth and tapped its ash away. 'I've never known one of them to be on time.'

'Yep. It sure is unusual.' Howard swallowed hard. 'The last time that happened a whole herd of Apaches from south of the border was on the rampage. We never did find out what happened to that stage or any of the folks that was travelling in it. All we found was arrows and a heap of bloodstained sand five miles yonder.'

'There much trouble with Apaches in these parts, son?'

Howard rubbed his neck. 'Nope. There ain't bin no Injuns of any sort in these parts for years. That's why I'm wondering what happened to the stage. It don't make no sense. No sense at all.'

'Where was it coming from?' Hickok took a long drag of smoke into his lungs and turned his head to stare at the towering wall of rock that loomed close behind them.

'Same place as you come from yesterday,' Howard replied. 'Rio Hondo and beyond.'

'And it never showed?' Hickok thought about the situation as he continued to stare out at the lofty wall of rocks.

'Where the hell is it?'

Hickok rested his hip on the parapet. His hooded eyes still watched the mountain range and the high mesas. 'Probably had itself an accident. That ground is rough out there. Sure shook my bones loose. Reckon it broke an axle or something.'

'Maybe I ought to send out a rider to take a look,' Howard suggested. 'What ya reckon?'

'Sounds like a smart idea.' Hickok drew in more smoke and savoured its aroma. 'Shame ya ain't got no telegraph wires strung up. Saves an awful lotta saddle leather being able to wire folks. If'n ya had a telegraph ya could wire Rio Hondo and ask them if the stage left on time or not. For all you know the damn thing is sitting in a livery stable whilst its crew are getting liquored up.'

Howard nodded in agreement. 'Yep. Ya right. The company figures on putting up a telegraph line next summer. We sure could use one about now though.'

Hickok ran the palm of his left hand over his moustache. He looked every inch a hero in the eyes of his companion. There was something flamboyant in his every fibre. Howard could not even look at the man without recalling the dozens of stories he had read in dime novels.

'Did ya do all them things they say ya done in the books, Wild Bill?' Howard sounded like a child, his excitement in meeting his hero briefly overcasting his concern for his missing stagecoach.

'Some of them are true,' Hickok replied.

Howard noticed that his companion had not taken his eyes off the imposing mesas since he had reached the high parapet. He wondered why.

'What ya looking at, Wild Bill?' Howard asked curiously.

Hickok pulled back on his fringed buckskin jacket revealing a pair of holstered guns. They were crossed over his lean waist with their pearl handles jutting out above his buckle. Just like the novels said, this was the king of the cross-draw in all his glory.

'Them mesas. I once had me a mighty close call up in them rocks, Mr Howard.' Hickok said drily. 'Too close.'

Howard drew nearer. 'Was that one of ya adventures in them books about ya? Maybe I read about it.'

Hickok shook his mane of long brown hair off his face. His hooded eyes stared into those of the younger man.

'Nope. I never told no book writer about that.'

Howard raised his eyebrows. 'But why not?'

'Some things are best forgotten.'

'But what happened up there?' Howard pressed eagerly as the famous man began to descend towards the station grounds once again. 'Was it a shootout? Or maybe ya tussled with a bunch of Injuns? What?'

'I ain't spoke about it in all of the years since it happened, boy.' Hickok seemed to be reluctant to talk about the incident. 'It was the kinda thing ya try a lifetime to forget but it sorta haunts ya all the same.'

Howard followed the man whose long shadow stretched towards the station building. 'Ya gotta tell me. I've read everything they ever printed about ya over the years. Tell me. What happened up in them mesas?'

Wild Bill Hickok paused and looked at Howard. It was as if two arrows were burning into the manager's soul, but it did not stop the questioning.

'Please, Bill. Tell me. I'll never spill it to no living soul. I promise.'

'Most of them tales ya read about never happened.' Hickok said in a low drawl. 'They was made up by Eastern writers. Some of the stories were close to the truth but most were just yarns, Howard. Folks ate them up and them writers kept on dishing them out. Only Ned Buntline came close to trying to write the truth but the others were just making quick easy money.'

Howard led Hickok into the cool of the building and towards the bar. He grabbed a bottle of whiskey, pulled its cork and handed it to his guest. 'Here. Have a drink on me.'

'Ya want to know what really happened up in them mountains?'

'I surely do.'

'Then listen up.' Hickok poured three fingers of the amber liquor into a glass and lifted it up. He stared at the sunlight dancing through the whiskey before downing it. He set the glass down. 'It was twenty or more years back.'

Howard sat down next to the living legend.

'These parts were running red with blood,' Hickok recalled as he slowly refilled his glass. 'A critter was killing every damn person he come across, Howard. The rangers knew about my repu-tation as a tracker and asked if I might like to help them capture and kill the varmint. They offered me a tidy sum so I reckoned it would be an easy day's work for me. I was a tad more sprightly back then so I got me my best horse and headed on up into them mountains with every one of my guns and rifles.'

Rance Howard watched as a grey mist seemed to cloud over the eyes of the taller man.

'What happened then?'

'Took a while but I finally cornered him at a cave

mouth set directly under the tallest of them mesas. He never come out during the day and I found out why he only rode and killed during the night.'

'Who? Who was he and why did he only kill at night?'

Hickok sighed. 'They called him the Phantom, boy. His true handle was Axil Gunn. The most evil critter ever to set foot on this sand.'

'He was real?' Howard gasped. 'I heard about him but thought them stories were just eyewash.'

'Eyewash?' Hickok muttered before throwing the whiskey into his mouth and swallowing it. 'Yep. He was the realest bastard I ever faced. Had himself two sons by a Cree woman up in them caves set under the mountains. Some reckoned them caves led all over like rabbit warrens. Ya could travel a hundred miles through them without ever come out into the sun. That suited the Phantom just fine.'

'Why did he only come out at night to do his killing?' Howard probed. 'I don't understand.'

'He was an albino, boy.' Hickok snarled at the memory of the man's image as it flashed into his mind. 'Both his boys was the same. Not an ounce of colour in either of them. Like ghosts.'

'When ya cornered him, what happened?' Howard was eager to hear the answer but none came.

Hickok shook his head, grabbed the whiskey

bottle by its neck, turned and walked in the direction of the room he had rented.

Rance Howard heard the door slamming shut.

NINE

The sand was shifting. Moving as though it were alive beneath the hoofs of the two riders as they thundered along the well-used stagecoach trail towards Apache Springs. The shimmering haze before the pair of young mounts did not cause them to slow their pace. They responded beneath their new masters as Dix and Dan leaned over their saddle horns and urged them on. Mesas that almost touched heaven itself loomed like strange fingers pointing to a place that only eagles could reach with ease. A few miles ahead of them the riders started to see the dancing of light, which neither of them recognized.

Something was glistening on the sandy trail. Something was catching the blinding light of the overhead sun and sending out beams of warning. Both horsemen started to slow their horses by leaning back and hauling their reins up to their chests.

'Ya see that, Dixie?' Dan called out above the din of the pounding horses' hoofs.

'I see it,' Dix growled.

'What ya figure it is?'

'Damned if I know,' Dix answered.

It was sometime in the middle of the afternoon and they had been riding since an hour after dawn, when the young Johnny Parker had returned to Rio Hondo with two fine young horses in tow to replace the ones the Phantom had so mercilessly destroyed.

After what seemed an eternity the horsemen drew rein and continued along the dusty road on foot towards the strange object lying on the trail. Dix was first to drag a canteen from his saddle horn and unscrew its stopper. He swilled out his dry mouth and spat. His partner copied his actions.

The heat haze was taunting their eyes and their minds as both men kept trying to make out what was catching the sunlight ahead of them. Whatever it was it was blocking the road. They dropped to the ground and held their reins tightly as they moved closer to each other.

'What in tarnation is that?' Dan asked. He swallowed another mouthful of the warm water.

'Something big by the looks of it, Dan,' Dix replied, screwing up his eyes until they looked almost shut. 'Reckon we ain't gonna find us no answers until we gets closer.'

'We'd better water these nags before we does any-thing brave, Dixie,' Dan said. He removed his hat and dropped it on to the ground. He poured half the canteen's contents into its bowl and then watched as the young horse dropped its neck and started to drink.

'Good job I bought me a new hat.' Dix removed his Stetson and placed it down before his horse's legs. He used all of his precious liquid and filled its bowl. 'There weren't enough left of the one the Phantom shot off my head to water an ant with.'

Dan returned his canteen to the horn of his saddle and shook his head. 'I don't like the looks of that.'

'Something's dead,' Dix said.

Dan moved closer. 'Ya figure?'

Dix aimed a finger skyward at three large birds circling directly above the strange object ahead of them. 'Them buzzards smell themselves a free meal, Dan.'

The retired lawman looked up. 'Hell. I never even noticed them black bastards.'

Dix lifted his hat first and placed it on his grey head of hair. The droplets of water felt good to the man whose skin was the colour of burned leather.

'Are you as tuckered out as me, pard?' he asked. He held on to the saddle horn as he hung his canteen on to it.

Dan Shaw sighed heavily and rolled his eyes before he stooped and dragged his old Stetson off the sand. 'Ain't ya ever gonna ask me nothing smart, Dixie? Ya know I was plumb tuckered out before we even got to Rio Hondo. I ain't managed to get any less tuckered out. What ya reckon is dead up there?'

'Some poor varmint that probably bumped into the Phantom last night before sunrise.' Dix forced himself away from the lathered-up horse and walked to where his partner stood checking his bones.

'We've bin riding for hours and I ain't seen no hint of hoof tracks that Gunn might have left, Dixie. The only ones I seen have bin stagecoach wheel-rim and hoof tracks.'

'Yeah, I noticed them as well, pard.' Dix pulled his gloves tight over his hands. Then he noticed something ahead in the shimmering heat haze. 'We both seen that tall stallion Gunn was riding. There has to be tracks someplace. The ground sure ain't that hard.'

'Maybe his horse is a ghost like Gunn.' The veteran lawman laughed and then pointed. 'Damn it all. What *is* that up ahead, Dixie?'

'I ain't sure but I intend finding out.' Dix leapt up on to his saddle and swung the young horse full circle as his friend mounted. 'C'mon. A man could go grey waiting for you, Dan.'

Dan sat on his saddle, gathered his reins in his hands and shook his head. 'I hate to tell ya but we've both bin grey for the longest while.'

'C'mon.' Dix spurred and thundered towards the strange object which teased his tired eyes.

'Damn it all, Dixie.' Dan cracked his long leathers and forced his mount to follow.

The horsemen drove their mounts through the dry hot air towards whatever it was that they had spotted. As they drew closer they began to realize what it was.

Dix reined in to slow his mount and allow his partner to catch up with him. As his tall horse finally came to a halt there was no doubt in the gun-fighter's mind about what he was looking at. Once again they had been greeted by death. Dan hauled rein and then wrapped the leathers around his saddle horn.

'Not again,' Dan shouted angrily.

The stench swept over both riders as they fought with their horses only yards from the wreckage of the stagecoach and its dead.

Dan looked away. 'I'm getting kinda tired of this.'

'You and me both, pard.' Dix handed his reins across to his friend, dismounted quickly and started towards the crippled stagecoach lying on its side across the full width of the sandy road. All six of its horses were lying dead in their traces. A myriad flies were already feasting on the carcasses.

Like a man approaching his own gallows Dix slowed his pace as he reached the coach lying on its side. He stopped for a few moments and stared at the driver's seat. What was left of the shotgun guard hung by a leg caught on a broken metal bar. A bullet hole in his head was the only sign of what had happened to the man.

Dix vainly looked all around him for the driver. He turned to Dan, who was carefully guiding his horse to follow the gunfighter towards the mayhem.

'Can ya see the driver from up there, Dan?' Dix called out. 'He ain't here with the guard.'

'I'll take me a look.' Dan stood in his stirrups and started to survey the area.

The tired gunfighter was about to start walking again when he noticed the black metal box still lying behind the head of the dead guard. He moved close and then knelt. He dragged the hefty strong-box clear and looked at its padlock. It was intact.

'The strongbox is still here, Dan,' Dix called out as he rose to his full height. 'Still locked up tight.'

Dan rode up to him and stared down at the box at Dix's feet. 'Gotta be the work of the Phantom again, Dixie. No sane killer would leave a box full of money.'

Dix nodded in agreement. 'Yeah.'

Then Dan spotted something and tapped his spurs. The young horse trotted across the sand, then stopped as the scent of death filled its nostrils.

Dan gritted his teeth and looked down upon what was left of the stage driver. He had a bullet hole in his chest and was lying behind a clump of sagebrush.

'I found me the driver,' Dan shouted over his shoulder.

Dix clambered up and looked inside the body of the coach. Then he dropped back to the sand.

'There ain't no sign of passengers,' Dix called to his partner, who was approaching once more.

'I still don't savvy how Gunn can still be alive after all these years. Hell. We was darn young the last time he went on the warpath. He oughta be older than us by now.' Dan rubbed his face as if trying to wipe the scent of decaying bodies from his nostrils. The ex-marshal stopped his horse next to the coach.

'Yeah. It don't figure whichever way ya looks at it,' Dix said thoughtfully.

Dan shook his head. 'But this just gotta be the work of Axil Gunn, Dixie. Ain't it?'

'Yep.' Dix agreed. He lifted the strongbox up and eased it behind his partner's saddle cantle. He secured it with the bedroll leathers. 'Only a locobean leaves the prize behind but takes the time to kill half a dozen horses. It has to be Gunn.'

'The Phantom,' Dan corrected.

'I'm starting to get me a little worried about us going up against him again,' Dix admitted. 'We sure didn't do very well last time.'

Dan Shaw nodded. 'Yeah. He is kinda hard to kill.'

'Why strike at a stagecoach in the middle of the prairie for no better reason than to kill its crew and team?' Dix wondered as his gloved hands gripped the horn of his saddle.

'Maybe he was thinking old Wild Bill was aboard, Dixie,' Dan suggested. 'He's bin looking for him and someone might have said he was on a stage. Does that make any sense?'

'Maybe.' Dix threw himself up on to his saddle and forced his boot toes into his stirrups. 'If a madman can ever do anything that makes sense.'

Dan looked around the arid landscape which surrounded them and sighed. 'Where is he? Where'd ya reckon he went?'

'He's out there.' Dix aimed a finger at the line of mesas which stretched off in both directions for as far as they could see. 'He's hiding up in them mesas, I'll bet ya. Like a bear; I reckon he's hiding in a cave. Waiting there until sundown.'

Dan let out a noisy sigh, then rested a gloved hand on his saddle horn. 'How come he hides during the day, Dixie? What ya make of a critter that does that?'

Dix bit his cracked lower lip.

'He ain't got no choice, pard. It's his skin,' Dix said knowingly. 'He ain't got no colour in all of his worthless hide like normal critters. I've heard that them kinda people or even animals can't move around in the sun or their skin just burns clean off.'

Dan looked at his pal. 'Burns off?'

'Yep. Clean off. He gotta hide just like a stinking sidewinder until the sun sets again before he can carry on.'

'Like a stinking sidewinder.' Dan spat.

'C'mon.' Dix turned his horse. 'We gotta get to the station before sundown.'

'Ya figure Wild Bill is there, Dixie?'

'There's only one way to find out.'

Dan wrapped his reins around his gloves. 'Do ya think he knows this Phantom varmint, Dixie?'

Dix gave a slow nod. 'That don't matter none. The thing is the Phantom seems to know him. Axil Gunn seems to want to get his hands on Wild Bill and in my book that means only one thing.'

'Revenge?' Dan ventured.

'Yep.' Dix nodded.

Both horses responded to their masters' spurs as they were steered around the wrecked stagecoach and back on to the dusty road once again.

Shoulder to shoulder the riders thundered on towards the way station known as Apache Springs.

TEN

Heaven was ablaze above the prairie. The sky was crimson as though hell itself were sending out a warning to all those who might be riding beneath its vast fiery canopy once the sun had finally decided to set. The high rocky pinnacles looked as though waves of fire were lashing up their towering surfaces. The day was ending but it was putting on a display that had style. Only those who had ridden this remote parched land would ever have witnessed the way days died in this region. No devilish inferno could equal the sight of that which surrounded the two riders as they forged relentlessly on. It was as though the gods themselves were fighting. As always it would be night that eventually prevailed, triumphant.

Dix and Dan knew that time was running out if they were to reach the way station before darkness swept across Apache Springs and engulfed them.

The two horsemen refused to allow their aged bones to slow the pace they demanded from their mounts. They could see the distant adobe building catching the final rays of the setting sun across its sturdy walls. There seemed to be no sign of life to the riders as they whipped their long leathers across the tails of their horses.

There was no time to fret about anything except reaching the one place between Rio Hondo and Cactus Flats where men might seek and find sanctuary.

The horses beneath them might have been young but they were also spent. Yet for all their weariness the two young mounts obeyed their new masters and somehow managed to keep finding renewed pace. Dust rose up into the air above the thundering riders as they kept forcing their charges on towards the way station. Darkness had not arrived but it was not far off. The eyes of both horsemen kept darting all around them, seeking out the deadly man they had already encountered once. If the man who called himself the Phantom was anywhere close they would see his dust.

Even ghosts could not ride across this terrain without dust being kicked up off his mount's hoofs.

The station came closer with every beat of the two veteran riders' hearts. All they had to do was keep going and ride into the courtyard of the solitary building that faced them. Ride in and get the gates closed and secured.

Dix slowed his pace and allowed his partner to ride ahead of him. The gunfighter realized that Dan had been burdened with the weight of the strongbox tethered to his saddle cantle. Dix drew one of his weapons and cocked its hammer as he rode behind the still galloping horse of his friend. If the Phantom even raised his head above the sagebrush Dix had secretly vowed to himself that he would blow it clean off the killer's shoulders.

Dan was swaying on his saddle as all exhausted men tend to do when riding. Dix trailed him as they came ever nearer to the wide-open gates of the station.

Suddenly, as they got within a half mile of the high walls Dix began to feel sweat trickle down his spine beneath his shirt and coat. A thousand fears exploded in his tired mind.

What if there was no one left alive in the way station?

What if Axil Gunn had already been here?

What if he and his tired pal were thundering towards another scene of misery?

What if the Phantom was waiting for them?

Waiting to finish what he had started the night before at Rio Hondo. Dix dropped down on to his saddle and thrust both spurs into the flanks of his mount. Within seconds the tall horse had caught up with Dan's mount.

Dix waved his hand at the exhausted former lawman. Dan's eyes darted to his partner.

'What?' Dan yelled out above the sound of their horses' pounding hoofs.

'Stop!' Dix yelled.

Never a man to argue with his friend Dan drew rein.

Both the sweating horses stopped within a hundred yards of the way station and watched their dust continue on towards its wide-open gates.

'What's wrong, Dixie?' Dan gasped, panting like an old hound dog. 'We're nearly there.'

Dix eased his horse next to that of his friend and pointed straight ahead of them. Dan followed the aim of his partner's gloved finger as it moved across the image of the building before them.

'What ya seen?' Dan asked.

'I ain't seen nothing, Dan boy,' Dix whispered in a low drawl. 'But by my reckoning we ought to be seeing somebody on them walls.'

Dan removed his hat and rubbed his temple dry on the back of his coat sleeve. 'Tell me again. Why'd we damn well stop?'

'Had me a thought,' Dix answered. 'What if Gunn is waiting for us in there?'

Suddenly Dan Shaw looked as though his brain had awoken. He squinted through the red illumination of the setting sun at the station and felt his throat tighten as though a noose had been pulled around his neck.

'I never give that a thought,' Dan muttered fearfully. He rested his hand on his gun grip.

'We'd be sitting targets once we rode in if he is in there waiting for us,' Dix added.

Then both men saw a torch being lit on the highest point of the wall ahead of them. The shimmering image of a man moving on the parapet taunted their dust-filled eyes.

'Somebody's in there OK.' Dan licked his dry lips. 'Can ya make him out, Dixie boy?'

Dix screwed up his wrinkled eyes. 'I can see someone on that wall but I can't make out who it is.'

Then oil lanterns burst into light deep in the courtyard beyond the open gateway. The shape of the station building became clear.

'There's more than one of them inside the walls of that place,' Dan observed with a sweep of his hand. 'One up on the wall and another lighting lanterns.'

Dix felt his every fibre relax. 'Then it can't be the Phanton inside the station, Dan. Not if there's at least two of them.'

Dan nodded. 'Ya right. That Gunn varmint don't seem to cotton to having company.'

Tom Dix was about to speak again when he saw a rider emerge from between the open gates. The sun was almost gone but there was enough blood-coloured light to dance upon the rider who was slowly approaching them.

'Who is that, Dixie?' Dan stammered. 'Looks like the Devil himself.'

Dix raised his gun and rested it on his saddle horn.

'Whoever it is he's riding straight towards us, old friend.'

Dan tried to swallow. He could not find the spittle.

ELEVEN

The defiant sun fell at last below the distant mountain range, leaving only shadows in its wake across the prairie. The sky quickly faded from its scarlet hue into a dark void which made the approaching rider appear even more ominous to Tom Dix and Dan Shaw. The moon was still low and had not yet started to compete with the countless stars which covered the vast eanopy of black velvet above Apache Springs. The way station's torch and lantern lights made the silent horseman seem as though he were riding out from the gates of Hell itself. The two trail-weary riders held their mounts in check as the lone horse and its master came closer and closer.

Neither Dix nor Dan could make out any of his features as he kept the horse walking straight towards them. A hundred thoughts raced through both men's minds as they watched the rider elegantly steer the muscular stallion away from the open gateway right at them.

His heart racing, Dan leaned away from his horse until he was close to his silent partner.

'Is that him, Dixie?' Dan whispered. 'Is that Axil Gunn?'

For what felt like a lifetime to the frightened ex-marshal his friend said nothing at all. He just kept staring directly at the rider watching his every move-ment.

Dan felt the sweat inside his gloved hand as it rested upon the grip of his holstered six-shooter. He screwed up his eyes but could not make out any detail on the rider who kept his mount moving to close the distance between them.

'Say something, Dixie,' Dan urged. 'Is that the critter we've bin chasing all of these miles? Is it the Phantom? Is it?'

Dix ignored his partner's questions.

He just kept staring with unblinking eyes at the man who showed no fear as he approached. The seasoned gunfighter had faced many men in his time and knew that to blink for even a brief second gave your adversary the chance to draw and shoot. It was an error renowned gunfighter Tom Dix had never made, and one that he did not intend making now.

Dan was getting more and more agitated.

'I'm gonna kill him if he moves even one of his

hands.' Dan slid his gun from its holster anxiously. His thumb eased back on its hammer until it locked into position.

'I'd not try to kill him if I was you, pard,' Dix said from the corner of his mouth.

'What?' Dan turned his head and stared through the darkness at the side of his friend's face. Dix was still staring straight ahead at the rider who kept on coming. 'Why shouldn't I try and kill him, Dixie?'

'Because if ya try he'll surely kill ya,' Dix muttered.

'How do ya know that?' Dan snapped.

'Because that's not the Phantom.' Dix sighed as he recognized the rider. 'That's our old pal Mr Hickok. I've seen both of ya handle ya guns many times and my money surely ain't on you winning a showdown, Dan.'

'Wild Bill?' Dan's head swung back to look at the horseman who was pulling back on his leathers until his handsome mount stopped. Dan screwed up his eyes and leaned over the neck of his horse. 'Are ya sure?'

The horseman remained like a statue on his mount. He said nothing as his hands cupped the flame of a match and raised it to a long thin cigar gripped between his teeth. As the glowing flame of the match lit up his features both riders could see the distinctive countenance clearly.

'Ya getting old, Dan. Ya never used to be jumpy,'

Hickok said through a line of smoke. 'I recall when ya had vinegar.'

'Damn it all, Bill.' Dan released the hammer and dropped his .45 back into its holster. 'Ya scared me half to death. I'm too tuckered to be spooked like that. What ya doing coming out from the station like that?'

'The manager lost himself a stagecoach this morning and I was figuring on taking me a look to see if I could find it.' Hickok inhaled on his cigar. 'I plumb forgot about you boys.'

Dix smiled. 'Figures.'

'Howdy, Dixie,' Hickok said, tilting his head. 'Howdy, Daniel.'

'James Butler Hickok,' Dix acknowledged. 'We heard ya got run out of Rio Hondo.'

Hickok gave a gruff laugh. 'Anybody would think I was trouble the way they treated me, Dixie.'

Dan scratched his whiskers and looked hard at Dix. 'Say. How'd ya know it weren't the Phantom, Dixie?'

Before Dix had time to explain Hickok tapped his spurs and made his horse move right up to those of his friends. He pulled the cigar from his mouth and stared at Dan. Even the eerie light of the moon and stars could not hide the urgency in his normally poker-faced expression.

'The Phantom?' Hickok repeated the name.

'Easy, Bill,' Dan said.

'What's wrong, James Butler?' Dix wondered.

Hickok forced his horse forward until it was between those of his two oldest pals and grabbed Dan's sleeve.

'Did I hear ya right? Did ya say something about the Phantom, Dan? Did ya?'

Dan nodded slowly. 'Sure did. We bin chasing the varmint after he done killed a whole bunch of folks back at Rio Hondo. We had us a tussle with him but he escaped after killing our nags.'

'Can't be the Phantom. It just can't,' Hickok hissed with a snarl. He dragged his reins around, then spurred. The stallion bolted back towards the flickering lights of the way station as the two befuddled riders followed. All three rode in through the open gates as Rance Howard came walking from the stables with one of his men at his elbow. Hickok kept riding until he reached the entrance to the building and dismounted swiftly. He marched into the lantern light.

Just inside the station Dix drew rein and looked at both of the men who had emerged from the stable.

'Ya best get them gates locked up tight, friends,' Dix advised.

'What for?' Howard stopped in his tracks as he saw the strongbox on the back of Dan's saddle. He pointed. 'What you two galoots got that box for? That's meant to be on the dawn stage from Rio Hondo.'

Dix had seen Hickok stop his horse outside the long building and dismount. The gunfighter dropped from his high-shouldered horse and walked up to the station manager. There was fury in his eyes.

'Listen up. Get them damn gates locked up tight, son,' Dix growled. 'There's trouble coming. Bad trouble. Lock them gates. Now.'

Howard indicated to the man beside him. 'Do it, Sam. Lock both of them gates up tight like the old-timer said.'

The man ran to the nearer gate and started to close it.

'Ya still ain't answered me,' Howard pressed as Dan stopped his horse next to the fence poles of the corral. 'How come ya got the strongbox?'

'We plucked it out of the stage up yonder, young 'un.' Dan eased himself off his horse and started to unravel the leather laces holding the hefty box in place. 'Figured if we left it there somebody less honest than us might find and take it.'

There was a terrified gasp from Howard when the gravity of the situation dawned on him. 'Hell. Ya mean something's happened to the stage?'

'Yep.' Dix nodded and stood within spitting distance of the younger man. 'We found it on its side about five miles back with both driver and guard shot dead. All of the horses were dead as well. Does that answer ya damn questions, boy? Does it?'

Dan dropped the box at Howard's feet. 'Easy, Dix.'

'Rub our horses down. We'll more than likely be needing them.' Dix swung around and strode away from Howard towards the long adobe building, which he had seen Hickok enter. The sound of the gunfighter's spurs rang out around the courtyard.

Rance Howard bent over and lifted the box up off the sand and then looked at Dan hard and long. 'What's going on, mister? Are there bandits out there about to attack the way station?'

Dan patted the arm of the manager. 'Follow me. I'll explain when Wild Bill has cleared up a few things for me.'

Howard started to follow, then turned back. 'Rub down these men's horses, Sam,' he ordered, 'Once ya get both gates locked up tight, that is.'

'OK, Rance.' The muscular man touched his hat brim and set off to run the distance to the other gate.

'Are we gonna be attacked?' Howard repeated.

Dan Shaw mounted the boardwalk outside the open doorway to the main room of the building. He paused and glanced at the trembling man beside him.

'Could be. Let's just say that we just might be in a whole heap of trouble, son,' he drawled. He entered the brightly illuminated room where he could see Dix and Hickok propped up against the bar.

111

'Hell!' Howard cursed before staggering after the dust-caked rider, carrying the heavy strongbox in his arms. 'Some days I wish I'd listened to my ma and become a damn teacher.'

Just as Howard reached the three men standing at the bar counter Hickok turned and faced him.

'Ya got any guns and rifles in this station, Howard?' he asked.

The station manager nodded. 'Yep.'

'Then dig them out, boy, and as much ammunition as ya can lay ya paws on,' Hickok ordered.

The station manager placed the strongbox on a table, clenched both hands into fists and stomped his right boot on to the boarded floor like an irate child.

'Ain't one of ya old fossils gonna tell me what's going on here?'

TWELVE

Rance Howard did not get any of the answers he sought from the men who remained silent and propping up his bar counter. Frustrated, the young way station manager marched off to where he kept the small arsenal of weaponry and ammunition provided by the Overland Stagecoach Company for the protection of its property and passengers. There was a silence between the three men who leaned on the bar counter. A silence pregnant with unanswered questions and brooding thoughts. The only sound came from the pouring of whiskey into three thimble glasses as the tall elegant man with the flowing long hair did what he always did when troubled, and sought refuge in a bottle of hard liquor. His two friends watched him as he lowered the bottle and then took hold of the tiny glass.

Hickok raised the glass and downed its fiery contents in one throw. Dix sipped at the amber liquor whilst Dan toyed with the glass on the damp wooden surface before him.

At last Dix spoke.

'Listen up. How come ya got so spooked by the name of the Phantom, James Butler?'

Hickok's eyes narrowed. He filled his glass again and stared at its contents the way he always stared at well-rounded females. 'I ain't spooked, Dixie. I'm just damn confused.'

'Why are ya confused?' Dix finished his whiskey and pushed his empty glass towards his friend, who refilled it.

'It's a long story, old friend.' Hickok went to lift his glass and then seemed to change his mind. He turned and rested his back against the counter and stared at the large room with dead eyes. 'An awful long story.'

'I like long stories,' Dix quipped.

'My long story don't make no sense,' Hickok replied.

Dan swallowed his drink and sighed. 'I knew that ya must know of this Phantom critter, Bill. I told Dixie that after we learned of him killing all them folks back at Rio Hondo, after he done asked folks if they'd seen ya. I said that he must really hate ya and was looking for revenge for something you must have done to him.'

Hickok glanced at Dan. 'This critter that calls himself the Phantom was asking about me?'

Dix downed his whiskey and placed his glass on

the bar. 'He sure was, and got real ornery when they told him that you had left town. That's when he started killing.'

The tall man with the fringed buckskin coat walked away from the bar to stand before the roaring fire and rested a boot on its stone hearth. The light of the fire danced across his totally expressionless features.

'Can't be the Phantom,' Hickok said without looking at his companions, who had joined him beside the fire. 'Whoever it was it sure can't be the Phantom, boys.'

'Damn it all. We seen him. We fought with him,' Dix argued. 'It was the Phantom OK. I met Axil Gunn twenty or more years back and he ain't a critter a man forgets in a hurry. It was the Phantom. I'd bet my saddle on it.'

'Then you'd be riding bareback, Dixie,' Hickok drawled.

'It was him,' Dix insisted.

Hickok moved his head. 'I'm telling ya, Dixie. It can't be him. It can't be Axil Gunn ya seen and fought.'

Dan pointed a finger at Hickok. 'No? He wrote his name in blood on saloon mirrors after he'd slaughtered a heap of folks, Bill. He wrote "The Phantom".'

'It can't be him, I'm telling ya,' Hickok protested loudly.

At just that moment Howard returned to the main room of the station laden down with an armful of rifles, handguns and boxes of ammunition. He placed it all down on the top of one of the tables and looked at the three men by the fire.

'Who can't be who?' Howard asked.

'Hush up, young 'un,' Dan snapped.

Rance Howard sat down and sighed.

'Why can't it be him, James Butler?' Dix asked. 'Why are ya so darn sure that we're wrong? We saw Axil Gunn. He killed both our horses and nearly done for us as well. It was him. White skin. White hair and beard. Black glasses. Ya wrong. It was definitely the Phantom. Nobody else looks like that.'

Hickok shook his head. 'Wrong again.'

'Ya mean there somebody else that looks the way Axil Gunn looks, James Butler?' Dix could not take his eyes off the troubled man. 'Are ya serious?'

Hickok stood upright. His hooded eyes burned into his two friends like red-hot pokers.

'I'm dead serious. He had himself two sons by a Cree woman and both them boys looked like Gunn. Like they'd bin washed in bleach and left out in the sun to dry.'

Dix stepped up to Hickok until their vest buttons touched.

'Convince me that Dan and me are wrong,' Dix insisted. 'I'm saying that was the real genuine Phantom. He might have had himself a couple of sons but Gunn was loco and whoever it is killing his way across the south-west is also loco. It has to be Axil Gunn.'

James Butler Hickok pulled his guns free of their holsters and held them out for both men to stare at. The weapons gleamed in the light of the fire's flames.

'See these hoglegs?'

Dix and Dan nodded.

'I killed Axil Gunn with these beauties,' stated Hickok.

Dix reached out and touched the guns in his friend's hands. 'Ya killed him?'

'Yep. More than twenty years ago I hunted him up into them hills and we had us a battle. A war. It lasted for over three hours, boys. Both of us was shot up real bad but I got the better of him.'

'Ya killed Axil Gunn?' Dix repeated.

'Ya killed the Phantom?' Dan almost echoed.

'Yep.' Hickok nodded. 'I blew his head clean off with these very guns. I left his carcass in the mouth of one of those caves set up in the rocks. Left it there for the buzzards.'

'Ya said he had himself a Cree woman and two sons?' Dan chewed on his thoughts. 'What happened to them during this bloody battle?'

'They run off like scared rabbits into the caves up there,' Hickok recalled. 'I never gave them no thought after I'd finished my job. I was bleeding

117

like a stuck pig and had to get to a doctor damn fast and have myself tended. I was carrying two of his bullets and I wanted them cut out.'

Dix walked back to the bar,' refilled his glass and downed the whiskey in one throw. He turned and stared hard at the troubled Hickok. For the first time he knew why the tall man was so confused. 'Then, if Axil Gunn is dead. . . ?'

'Who the hell did we see?' Dan gulped.

'Who has bin doing all the killing?'

Hickok holstered his guns and ran his fingers through his mane of long hair. 'And who in tarnation is calling himself the Phantom?'

'It has to be one of his sons,' Dix said confidently. 'There ain't no other answer I can figure.'

'Bent on revenge,' Dan opined with a shrug. 'Revenge for what ya done to his pa, Bill.'

'He must be as crazy as his pa was,' Dix surmised.

Hickok gave a slow nod. 'Yep. Looks like I got me another Phantom to kill, boys. I have to finish the job I started twenty sum years back. I gotta kill the Phantom all over again before anyone else gets themselves shot up by this varmint.'

'Ya wrong, James Butler.' Dix walked back to his pal.

'How am I wrong, Dixie?'

'Ya ain't taking him on all on ya lonesome. I'm tagging along with ya, James Butler.' Dix rested his hands on his holstered pair of matched .45s. 'I'll make sure ya does it right this time.'

'Damn it all.' Dan removed his hat and beat the dust off against his leg. 'I can't let you two hotheads go without me covering ya backs.'

Hickok smiled. 'You boys still got vinegar.'

THIRTEEN

The range of mesas loomed like strange nightmarish monsters above the prairie in the darkness. Yet there was a real monster hidden somewhere amid the craggy boulders and rocks. A monster in human form, who was far more deadly than any mythical creation. This was the home of the man who insanely called himself the Phantom. This was his territory. The place that had spawned him. As the night progressed it grew ever darker as black storm clouds gathered in the heavens and slowly began to cover every star and the usually bright prairie moon.

Chilling coyote cries echoed all around the arid terrain and the high cliffs. A cloud of insects kept up their nightly ceremonial hullabaloo all around the intrepid rangers who slowly entered the most dangerous section of the unforgiving prairie carrying their blazing torches high overhead. The line of fearless horsemen had been riding since dawn and were prepared to continue their quest until it was resolved.

They had all accepted their leader's pledge. They would not quit their hunt for the brutal Phantom until either he or they were dead. To men like the stalwart rangers there was simply no other way. They knew that the coming of nightfall meant their adversary was on the rampage. He would be killing all who had the misfortune to get in his way. Captain Jones knew that there was only one way to get the better of a maniac and that was to think like a madman.

He knew that it was insanity to keep riding when you, your men and your horses were totally exhausted, but that was the only way anyone had a chance of besting the creature who called himself the Phantom.

The strange sight of the line of glowing torches might have frightened off usual prey, but Jones felt sure that it might just have the opposite effect on a madman. It might just lure the Phantom out of his hiding-place.

Captain Jones was convinced that that was the only way he and his rangers had a hope of coming face to face with the deranged butcher who had eluded them for so long. He had to be tempted from his lair and then swiftly dispatched.

This was a venomous creature who did not

deserve to captured alive and then put on trial. The Phantom had to die in order to save the lives of countless innocents he might yet encounter.

The advancing riders rode in a wide line across the wild, untamed land, holding their fiery torches aloft. Dust rose up above the tired horses and their masters as the rangers forged their way through the hazardous terrain.

As they rode beneath the high wall of rock each of the rangers pondered the same thought. Would the mysterious Phantom be drawn towards their strange illumination? Like a moth to a naked flame? Would he be tempted to try his luck with men who were highly trained, unlike his usual victims who were rarely even armed?

The Texas Rangers had only stopped their relentless riding at hourly intervals to water and feed their horses since they had left Blake's Ridge. They had ridden in a straight line across the landscape, hoping that by not taking the stagecoach road they might just manage to get ahead of their prey, or at least draw level with him.

It was a gamble but Captain Bodie Jones had always enjoyed taking risks. His stalwart men would follow loyally wherever he led them. They all knew that if there was a fight on hand then Jones would be at the head of his troop of men. He had never asked any of them to go where he was not willing to go first.

The rangers realized that their horses were physically spent but they refused to rest for more than a few minutes every hour, to water the animals. This was their last chance to get the better of the Phantom.

This was do or die and each of them was willing to make the ultimate sacrifice.

This was their last chance to end the brutal maniac's reign of terror and bloodshed.

Since leaving Blake's Ridge they had carved out a direct route across the prairie. Unknown to them, they had gained on the killer they pursued.

For the first time since leaving Badwater they unknowingly had the advantage on the man they hunted. The pack of hounds had at last managed to catch up with the fox, yet they had no idea how close they actually were.

His scent was in their flared nostrils.

Then as the dust-caked rangers rode in line, with their torches blazing between huge boulders at the foot of the first in the long line of cliffs and towering mesas Captain Jones saw something beyond the sagebrush. Something was caught in the flickering light of their torches.

He raised an arm and drew rein. The rangers all stopped beside him.

'What is it, Captain?' Toby Hope asked as he steadied his mount next to that of his leader. 'What ya seen?'

'There.' Excitedly Jones pointed at the ground. 'Do ya see it, Toby? Look, boys.'

Toby Hope swung his horse around and balanced on his left stirrup. His old eyes peered down through the darkness as Jones held out his torch to cast light down on the distinctive marks of a shod horse imprinted in the sand.

'I see it.' Hope gasped. 'We done found his tracks. If'n they is his tracks, that is.'

'Who else would be riding in these parts, Toby?' Jones laughed. 'They're his all right and they're mighty fresh. Look at the sand where its dampness has bin kicked up. Ain't even had time to dry.'

'Ya plan has panned out,' one of the rangers said.

'It was real risky but ya got it right,' another added.

'I knew he weren't using the road,' Jones said through gritted teeth. 'I knew the bastard was riding like them old crows fly. Straight like an arrow. That's why we ain't bin able to catch him. Until now. Now we got him.'

The rest of the rangers patted the necks of their mounts and started to talk feverishly to one another. They all scowled at the hoof tracks of the Phantom's horse.

'He can't be far ahead, Captain,' one of the rangers named Boyd Farmer said with a chuckle. 'How far do ya figure he is, Captain?'

'I reckon he ain't more than a mile ahead of us.'

Jones screwed up his eyes and looked at the black mountains, considering their situation. 'I bet ya all a steak dinner that he can see our torches right now from one of them caves that riddles these old mountains!'

'I sure hope he's good and scared,' one of the other rangers snarled.

'Even locobeans get scared when they see a herd of Texas Rangers on their tail,' Hope joked loudly. 'Ain't that right, Bodie boy?'

'Damn right, Toby,' Jones agreed. 'He's probably shaking in his boots wondering how long it'll take us to get his worthless hide in our sights.'

The storm clouds high above them parted for a few brief moments, allowing the light of the moon to cast down upon the prairie. What it revealed chilled and stunned every one of the rangers.

Boyd Farmer pointed his torch ahead of them to where a series of boulders rested in a line. Then screamed out in shock.

'Look.'

Every horseman looked.

Every one of them gasped in horror.

There sitting astride his grey stallion less than 200 yards ahead of them the creature they were hunting was looking straight at them with both his cocked six-shooters gripped in his hands. Like a ghostly apparition the merciless Phantom just sat watching the rangers, like a man choosing a turkey for his

Thanksgiving dinner.

Bodie Jones's eyes opened wide as he, like his men, stared at the unearthly horseman who defiantly faced them.

'It's him!' he gasped in disbelief.

A concerted gasp swept through the rank of the rangers like a gust of wind. For a few fleeting moments they could see the Phantom quite clearly.

Then the black clouds returned to cover the moon and stars once more. The terrifying image vanished from view.

'What ya waiting for?' Jones yelled out at the top of his voice. He drew his pistol from its holster and cocked its hammer. 'Fire.'

Yet before any of them had time to obey his order and raise their guns a deafening clamour filled all their ears as red-hot tapers came speeding towards them from where they had caught a fleeting glimpse of the Phantom.

It was raining bullets and all of them were coming from one direction: from the boulders where the deadly killer had mocked them so defiantly.

The screams of his men filled Jones's ears. The ear-splitting bullets kept on coming, driving into his torch-wielding rangers like a swarm of lethal hornets dishing out stings of hot lead.

Then Jones felt the impact aa a bullet hit him hard. He buckled, dropped his torch yet still somehow managed to squeeze his trigger. With his men falling all around him Jones hauled back on his hammer again and sent another feeble bullet back at the source of the unceasing bombardment.

'Keep firing, men,' Captain Jones managed to cry when his horse reared up and gave a plaintive whinny. Like its master it had been hit. The horse staggered as its hoofs returned to the sand. More bullets came racing in on the rangers. Jones felt his horse falling. Somehow he threw himself clear as the stricken animal crashed into the sand next to several still-flaming torches amid dead and dying men. Captain Jones had hit the ground hard but still managed to cock his gun once again and fire it.

His left arm was pumping blood where the bullet had shattered its bone. Jones could feel his heart pounding inside his bruised and battered torso. He stared in horror all around him. One by one all of his rangers were being blasted from their saddles and were crashing into the sand. The torches had made them sitting ducks for the man who was clearly an expert with his weaponry. The Phantom was killing them at will.

It was a turkey shoot and the rangers had been the turkeys.

Painful screams grew louder than the sound of gunfire.

Most were choking on their own blood as those who were not dead still tried to return fire.

127

For the umpteenth time the Phantom paused for a few seconds to reload.

Bodie Jones scrambled on to his knees and looked all around him in despair. Torches lay on the ground all about him. Their flames were highlighting the dead and wounded rangers. None of them remained on their mounts. Most of their horses were also either wounded or dead, lying beside their masters.

'Toby?' Jones called out to his friend as the shooting started again. The darkness lit up as the tapers of red-hot death returned to claim the lives of those who had somehow survived the initial volley. 'Are ya OK, Toby?'

Toby Hope did not answer.

Soon none of the other rangers was able to answer.

Captain Jones coughed and forced himself upright. His smoking gun hung in his hand by his side as he began to stagger forward to where he and his now dead men had seen the brief but memorable image of the Phantom.

'I ain't feared of ya,' Jones screamed out, slowly raising his gun to hip level. 'I ain't scared of no madman.'

There was just one more shot.

It did not come from the ranger captain's gun.

It came from the shadows. The bullet was perfectly placed between Jones's eyes. His boots lifted off the sand and he flew backwards. He landed on his back beside his comrades. His arm gradually fell on to his belly, still holding on to his smoking .45.

As the moon briefly appeared once more the dead eyes of Bodie Jones stared up at it. Then the sound of horses' hoofs filled the scene of carnage as the deathly white rider drew up to inspect his latest handiwork. The eyes hidden behind the black circles of glass surveyed the scene.

The Phantom made no sound. Somehow he had managed to get the better of them. The albino creature with the white skin and white beard displayed no emotion.

No hint of either regret or pleasure.

To him this was what he did.

He killed.

The Phantom shook his spent casings from his smoking guns and then reloaded them. When he was convinced that everything before him was dead he dropped the guns into their holsters and gathered up his reins.

He swung his grey stallion round and mercilessly drove his spurs into its flanks. Dust rose up from its hoofs as its master thundered away up towards the mountains above the scene of carnage.

The high parapet of the way station was a lonely place at the best of times, but after hearing the devilish sound of distant gunfire it became a truly terrifying one to Rance Howard. Only twenty minutes earlier he had watched Hickok lead Dix and Dan away from the relative safety of the way station and out into the eerie darkness, towards the mountains. With the echoes of the brief but bloody battle still resonating around the adobe walls the young station manager began to wish the three men were still at his side.

Howard knew now that he was alone, apart from his tiny staff of two men and one woman. None of them had an inkling of what was actually happening out there on the prairie, or that it might head in their direction at any moment. Clenching his fists as he cradled the rifle Howard silently cursed the darkness. At least during the day you could see your attackers even if you could do nothing to stop them. Night only offered shadows. Shadows amongst which the most evil of men might choose to conceal themselves.

He shuddered and tried to remain calm. He wondered if the sound of gunfire might make Hickok and his friends return to the station but Howard doubted it. They were not timid men who shied away from danger; they met it head on like mountain goats. They had no fear as he had. They would continue on to their goal. They had a course to navigate during the hours of dark shadows, one that would take them to the Phantom's lair.

A raucus chorus seemed to be mocking the

young man as he stared out at the vastness before him. The prairie was alive with unseen life. There were many creatures out there that could kill, but Howard feared only one of them: the one he had overheard Hickok and Dix talking about.

The Phantom.

Howard clutched the newly oiled Winchester and stared out into the blackness. All he could see were the nearby sagebrush and Joshua trees captured in the light of the two blazing torches to either side of the secured gates.

The flickering light only added to his fears as it danced on the parched vegetation. It was said that the brave are only men with little imagination. They never see the dangers others notice. To a man with a fertile imagination fuelled over the decades by reading countless dime novels, the dancing light evoked many visions.

Many frightening visions.

Howard had never been a troublesome man. He had always tried to use his wits rather than a gun to win his battles for him, but now, as the storm clouds rumbled ever more loudly above the way station he secretly wished that he had taken more interest in weaponry. He knew that if the stories of the Phantom were true and the unearthly being did show up none of his staff inside the walls of the way station stood much chance of surviving the meeting.

As Hickok had advised, Howard had issued them all with rifles in case they needed them to repel the Phantom.

Rods of lightning were flashing in the distance above the highest peaks of the mountain. Every few seconds Howard caught a tantalizing glimpse of the place for which the three riders were heading: the tall mesas.

Howard checked the weapon in his hands for the umpteenth time and was still not convinced that it was fully loaded. Sweat defied the cool breeze which cut across the prairie and ran down the face of the nervous man.

Doubts started to fester in his mind. There were only three other souls in the station. Would they be enough to fend off a murderous madman? None of them knew how to handle a gun. The clatter of the horses in the corral kept drawing Howard's attention as they raced around their fenced confines. They could smell the approaching storm and, like all sensible creatures, wanted to run in the opposite direction.

Howard had placed one of his stablemen on the west gate wall across the large yard. Jake Harper stood beneath the flames of one of the gate's torches, holding a rifle. Unlike his boss Harper was neither troubled nor afraid. Unlike Howard, the stableman had never read a book, had never fed his mind with stories of any kind.

All men like Jake Harper did was eat, drink, work and sleep. He was content. Nothing fanciful ever invaded his small world. He kept staring out at the trail waiting for the midnight stagecoach from Cactus Flats. He had heard Hickok and Dix talking about the ruthless killer who, they believed, was heading to the way station, but Jake Harper paid the idea no heed.

Howard paced along the parapet until he was directly above the stable. He called down. His other stablehand, named Sam Kane, was harnessing a team of fresh horses for the overdue stagecoach. It was the very same team he had harnessed hours earlier and had then released from their traces when he learned that the stage from Rio Hondo would never arrive.

'Sam,' Howard called down.

The burly man stepped out into the lantern light. His massive arms gleamed with a mixture of sweat and grease.

'What ya want, Rance?' Sam answered. 'I'm kinda busy here.'

'Ya got that rifle I give ya at hand?'

'Sure, but what do I want with a damn rifle?' The large man ran oily fingers through his thick dark hair. 'I don't know how to handle no carbine.'

'Neither do I but we might just have to learn if Hickok and the others are right about this place being attacked by that locobean.' Howard waved a finger. 'Keep that rifle close just in case. Ya hear me, Sam?'

'OK.' Sam sighed and walked back into the stable mumbling to himself. 'Don't go fretting none, Rance. I'll keep it close just in case we gets attacked by some dumb-ass idiot.'

Howard rose back to his feet and stared out again into the blackness which surrounded them.

The station manager licked his lips. They were dry. His throat was even drier. He needed a drink. A real stiff drink of whiskey, but the fearful man did not know whether he could leave his post. The three riders who had gone hunting for the Phantom had told him to stay put and remain alert.

But he was sure thirsty.

'I see the midnight stage coming, Rance,' Jake yelled out. 'Shall I open the gates?'

'Can ya see the driver's face, Jake?' Howard called back.

'I can see him just fine, Rance.'

'Do ya recognize him?'

'I surely do.'

Howard rubbed his neck. 'Then open the gates.'

Every thread of the station manager's clothing was drenched in his own sweat. He rubbed his face on his sleeve.

I sure could use me a long sip of whiskey right now, he thought, and sighed.

FOURTEEN

They had been riding ever upward for what felt like an eternity towards the grim walls of stone which had looked down on to the prairie for aeons. The black night sky above Apache Springs looked as though it were about to explode. Flashes of light erupted and moved faster than any eye could follow across the vast heavens somewhere above the brooding swirling clouds. Every few minutes deafening rolls and cracks of thunder shook the riders almost off their saddles and spooked their terrified mounts. Yet they forged on to where the brief flashes of light blinked across the ominous spires that rose amid the mesas. No monsters could have equalled the haunting sight. Mythical gods were warning the trio of intrepid horsemen to turn back before it was too late to do anything but die.

Yet James Butler Hickok, Tom Dix and Dan Shaw were not going to allow their gut instincts to prevail.

Not this night. Not this unholy night. They had a date with destiny itself and there was no way that any of them could do other than finish off the creature who had brought untold death to the borderland. They had to end the merciless reign of the man who called himself the Phantom. If they could achieve that daunting goal their lives would have been for a reason.

There was an ineffable power high above the three horsemen as they steered their mounts up through the perilous slopes of sand and rock. The heavens were alive and boasting of their power over all who dwelled beneath them. No mere mortal being could or would ever be able to muster such awe-inspiring potency as nature itself could. Rods of lightning were cutting down from erupting clouds and hitting the highest peaks of the long mountain range before them. It was like watching dynamite exploding but the riders kept tight rein and spurred hard.

Their eyes had taken a long time to adjust to the darkness of a cloud-filled sky. Now they could see everything before and above them. The stuttering light only aided their determined advance. Nothing could stop them now. Nothing but the bullets of the creature they hunted.

A million thoughts raced through their weary minds.

They each knew of the ancient legend of the

Phantom, of the tall stories that Axil Gunn had used to his advantage so many years before. Yet as they beheld the almost spectral peaks that rose among the mountains ahead of them they all began to wonder whether there might not just be some truth in them.

Some say that all legends and myths have their roots based in reality. What if this devilish land did harbour a real creature like the Phantom?

Then the rain started to fall. They felt its droplets hit their dusty faces, but they continued upwards to where Hickok had told them a series of caves existed; the caves where Axil Gunn and his family had lived so long ago. The renowned gambler was betting that whoever this new phantom was he was returning to where Axil Gunn had once lived. It was a long shot but Hickok was used to playing for high stakes.

The rain stung their weathered faces. The Apaches said that when it rained it was the Great Spirit weeping for what he saw men doing far below.

Were these the tears of a god? A god who pitied mere men taking on a beast created by Satan himself?

More flashes of lightning lit up the high rocks. They were nearing their destination and nothing would stop the riders from reaching it. They aimed their horses to where the mountains touched the sky and kept spurring.

Even the most loyal and obedient of horses needed more than a little encouragment to keep climbing in this desolate landscape.

Soft words could not cut the mustard here with tired, frightened horses. Only sharp spurs had the power to force them on towards the smell of sulphur spilling out from the storm's indignation.

The journey had been a long dangerous one and none of the trio expected to return unscathed. There was always a price to pay when you pitted yourself against another. What that price might be was known only to the gods themselves. Men were always the last to know what fate had in store for them.

Every so often Dix would rest his weight on his left stirrup, turn and look back at what lay behind and far below them. The only identifiable sight any-where on the vast prairie was the lights of the way station as they glowed softly in the blackness.

Ahead of them crags of rocks jutted out of the ground like giant playing-cards that had been embedded into the steep slope by some unimagin-able force. Hickok recognized the rocks from twenty years before. They were branded into his memory as the start of what had been his most dan-gerous adventure. He knew that they were now close to the caves. Caves that still had his dried blood covering the surface of their ancient walls.

For Hickok this was a return to a place he had thought he would never have to visit again. He had assumed that his business there had been finished long ago.

He now knew he had been wrong.

Damn wrong.

He looked up from beneath the flat brim of his hat as rain hit his distinctive features. A flash of lightning illuminated the entire mountain. Then blackness returned. But Hickok could still see the caves high above them. His blood chilled. This mountain was riddled with caves and he remembered how those very caves had almost cost him his life when he had fought with the Phantom.

Axil Gunn had used the caves to his advantage to get the drop on him. He recalled how they were all linked together, either by nature or by the labour of Gunn's own hands. A man could run into one cave entrance and then seemingly appear at the mouth of another as though by magic.

But there was no magic.

There was only the devilish mind of a maniac corrupted by evil. Hickok looked all around them as their horses reached the centre of a maze of craggy rocks a mere fifty or so feet below the caves. He pulled back on his reins and allowed his horse to turn to try and find level ground beneath its hoofs.

Dix slowed his horse and dismounted painfully. 'We gonna water the horses again, James Butler?'

'Let them drink the rain,' Hickok told him.

Dan stopped his skittish mount. 'Why'd we stop, Wild Bill?'

The sky erupted and blinding light swept like a tidal wave across the heavens above them. It flashed and flickered for a few seconds before the deafening thunderclap exploded above their heads.

Hickok turned his head and looked up.

'We're here,' he said in a low drawl.

Dix held his reins tightly, screwed up his eyes and tried to see what Hickok was looking at. 'I don't see nothing.'

'Me neither.' Dan eased himself off his horse and held the bridle of his mount. 'Ya said there are caves. I don't see me no caves.'

'Look harder.' Hickok raised a thin finger and pointed.

Both Dix and Dan looked harder.

'Damn it all.' Dix sighed.

'Yeah. I see them as well, Dixie.' Dan nodded.

Wild Bill Hickok dismounted and handed his reins to Dix. He paced over the ground, staring up at the steep slope that faced them. 'Gonna be a hard climb.'

'I'm just glad to be off that damn saddle,' Dan said. 'I reckon I ain't got me any skin left on my rump.'

Dix looked around them. 'We'll have to find someplace to tie these horses to. One more thunderclap and they'll be halfway to Mexico before we can spit.'

Hickok raised an arm. He did not look at where he was pointing. 'There are some old tree roots turned to stone just behind that boulder, Dixie. Secure them to those.'

'How can ya see what's behind that rock without even looking, Bill?' Dan asked as he gave his reins to Dix.

Hickok did not reply.

'He knows coz he was here twenty years ago, Dan,' Dix explained as he led the three horses to where Hickok had indicated. As the gunfighter rounded the corner of the large rock he stopped. 'Yep. It's still here, *amigos.*'

'Tie them firm, Dixie,' Hickok said.

Dan moved to the shoulder of the famed man. 'Ya figure we got us a chance against the likes of Axil Gunn, Bill?'

'It ain't Axil Gunn, Dan,' Hickok snapped. 'I killed Axil Gunn.'

'It's gotta be one of his boys,' Dix said. He rejoined his friends and patted Hickok's shoulder. 'Ain't that right, James Butler?'

Hickok nodded. 'Yep. That's right.'

'Whoever the Phantom is he'll surely try and kill us,' Dan said, and spat. 'Have we got even the slimmest of chances of bettering him, Wild Bill?'

Hickok had already killed the Phantom once and now he was going to try to do it again. If any

141

creature could be killed twice the tall man in the fringed buckskin jacket was willing to try.

'Ya gotta have faith, Dan. Just like playing poker. Ya just gotta have faith.'

'There ain't a lot of shooting when ya plays poker, Bill,' Dan said, checking his gun. 'This might get real bloody when we tangles with that bastard up there.'

Hickok looked at Dix and gave a wry smile from beneath his moustache.

'Danny boy here ain't seen the way I tend to play poker, has he Dixie?' Hickok observed as he started up the steep slope.

'He surely ain't, James Butler.' Dix nodded.

Dix and Dan followed Hickok.

The intrepid trio of men started to make their way up through the maze of rocks that led to the caves. The ground was wet and unstable but they continued on to where Hickok recalled that the Phantom had lived all those years previously. The rain began to ease, but the climb became no easier, as water flowed down the surface of the incline from the bases of the mesas. The men were having to use their hands as well as their feet in order to progress.

Then a blinding flash of lightning just above them erupted like a thousand sticks of dynamite. The men fell on their faces as the entire mountain beneath them shook. There was no gap between the lightning and the thunderclap. A rod of white death spirited down and hit the side of the highest rocky pinnacle. Debris of every size and shape burst over the three men as they clung to the slope. For what seemed like many seconds the rocks fell on and around them. Then there was silence again.

Eerie silence.

Hickok raised. his head first and cast his gaze back at the two men crouching just behind him.

'Are ya OK, boys?' he asked. Water continued to flow down over them.

Dix raised his head. 'I've bin better.'

'If that Phantom critter ain't hiding up here I'm gonna be mighty sore, Bill,' Dan grumbled.

All three had managed to scramble up again and resume their climb when two flashes followed by deafening gunshots came cutting through the rainfall from the ledge a mere twenty feet above them. The ground cut up just to the side of Hickok. Water and dirt kicked up into his hardened features.

'There he is,' Hickok yelled as lightning lit up the mountainside again in stuttering blasts of light.

Dix and Dan could see the deathly white gunman high above them holding his guns in his hands. Hickok cocked and fired at the gunman.

'Take cover, boys,' he ordered.

The two older men managed to move across the slippery surface of the slope until they were shielded by a jagged lump of rock jutting out of the slope.

143

'Get over here, Bill,' Dan pleaded with Hickok.

Another shot came hurtling down from the ridge as the Phantom ran into a cave behind him and disappeared from view. Hickok forced himself up on to his feet and steadied himself with his left hand whilst his right cocked his gun again and blasted up into the just visible cave entrance.

Both Dan and Dix watched in horror as Hickok cocked his gun yet again in readiness.

'Get over here, James Butler,' Dix yelled.

'You can hide like snivelling little gals if ya like.' Hickok glanced at them, then started to make his way up through the torrent of water towards the ridge. 'I'm for killing that critter.'

Dix looked at Dan. 'Ya coming?'

'Ain't got nothing better to do,' Dan answered and shrugged.

'Nothing except dying,' Dix added.

Both men drew their guns. They copied Hickok's actions and started to climb the last few yards up to where they had briefly caught sight of their deadly adversary.

Hickok was first to reach the ridge. His eyes surveyed the familiar place. The rocks of various shapes and sizes were still scattered all around the almost level patch of ground, as they had been twenty years earlier. Some were big enough for a man to take cover behind. Others were small enough to trip up a long-legged man and send him tumbling over the edge of the perilous perch, falling to his death.

The gunsmoke still lingered where the Phantom had fired his guns a few seconds earlier but the man himself was gone. Dix and Dan clambered over the lip of the ridge and forced themselves to stand upright next to Hickok, where he stood in his soaked fringed jacket.

'Where is he?' Dan asked, his gaze darting from one cave mouth to another. 'Damn it all. There must be over fifty holes on this lump of rock.'

'Forty-two to be exact,' Hickok corrected. 'I counted them a long time ago when the Phantom had me cornered behind that boulder yonder.'

All three men held their guns and kept looking from one black cave mouth to the next.

'Where is he?' Dix whispered. 'I seen him run into one of these caves, but which one was it?'

'It don't matter none,' Hickok drawled. He turned and aimed his six-shooter as the nearest of the cave entrances. 'Most of them are joined up, like I told ya. He could run in there and pop out over there. Keep them eyes peeled, boys. He'll surely kill ya if ya blink.'

The words had barely left his lips when suddenly the albino killer emerged to their right and fanned his gun hammer three times. Shafts of lethal lead came hurtling through the darkness at them.

Hickok swung around and knocked both his

companions off their feet just in time. The bullets hit a boulder situated on the very edge of the ridge. Sparks flew out in all directions as the three balls of lead ricocheted off the immovable object.

'How does he move so fast?' Dan wondered.

'Maybe he's younger than he looks,' Dix growled. While they had been lying on the ground both men had seen the incredible speed that Hickok still had with his guns. He had fired every bullet from his smoking weapon at the place where the mysterious character had been only a moment before. Hickok drew his other six-shooter and kept on firing.

But the Phantom was gone once more.

Hickok swiftly reloaded.

'Sorry about that,' he said as both his companions got back to their feet. 'You was standing in his line of fire.'

Dix watched in awe as Hickok snapped shut the chambers of both his guns and holstered one of the weapons. He had never in all his days seen anyone who could reload their guns as quickly as Hickok.

'Where'd he go?' Dix managed to ask.

'That ain't the question, Dixie,' Hickok told him. He walked closer to one of the cave entrances and squinted hard.

Both men moved next to him.

'What *is* the damn question, Bill?'

Wild Bill Hickok glanced at the retired lawman for a brief instant, then returned his attention to

146

the blackness inside the cave.

'The question is which one of these damn mouse-holes is he gonna poke his guns out of next,' Hickok answered. He sighed.

'Wish I had me a stick of dynamite,' Dan growled. 'I'd ram it right up his cave entrance and light the fuse.'

Hickok leaned back. 'I hear him running.'

Dix moved to the high shoulder. 'Yeah. I can hear his damn spurs jangling.'

With Dix and Dan right beside him, Hickok turned and paced to the next cave entrance, then to the next. He stopped and pointed his cocked gun into it.

'Look.'

Dix and Dan both looked into the darkness. For a few moments they saw nothing. Then, as their eyes adjusted, they spied the tall grey stallion tethered fifteen feet back.

'That's his horse,' Dan murmured.

Dix smiled. 'Cover me.'

Dan watched as Dix moved to the horse, who seemed quite unafraid. Dix raised the stirrup fender, and hooked it on to the saddle horn, then untied the cinch straps. He hauled the saddle off the back of the horse and dropped it on to the ground at his feet. The gunfighter was about to return to his two waiting comrades when he heard something behind him. Something deep in the cave tunnel.

147

He spun on his heels just as a trigger was squeezed in the depths of the cave. A bright flash lit up the cave walls as a shot came speeding towards him. Dix felt the heat of the lead as it cut through his jacket sleeve and ripped his flesh.

He yelled out in pain, stumbled, but managed to draw and fire his own Colt.

But the Phantom was gone again.

'Are ya OK, Dixie?' Dan called out.

'Yep. I guess so.' Dix grabbed his left arm and ran back to where his friends were waiting.

Hickok looked at Dix's injury. 'Ya just winged.'

'I figured that out myself, James Butler.' Dix groaned as Dan pulled his bandanna free and tied it just above the bloody hole in Dix's sleeve.

'That bastard is sure fast,' Dan said. He cast glances all around the many black cave entrances. 'What ya wanna go take a risk like that for, Dixie?'

'I figured that if the Phantom tried to hightail it he'd have to do it bareback, Dan,' Dix answered.

Hickok patted Dix's back. 'Good thinking. This ain't the sorta terrain to ride in without a saddle.'

Then the Phantom appeared from another of the cave mouths more than thirty feet away. Hickok pushed both Dan and Dix into the cave behind him as a spattering of shots came seeking them out. Each of the bullets hit the cave wall and sent dust showering over the three men.

'How'd he move so damn fast?' Dan asked again

as he fanned his gun hammer at a target which had already vanished back into the shadows. 'That's gotta be one hell of a run from where he winged Dixie.'

Wild Bill Hickok aimed a smoking barrel at the huge boulder that was less than ten feet from them. 'I want ya both to listen to me, boys. Listen and obey.'

'Sound like ya want to marry us, Bill.' Dan somehow laughed as he forced fresh bullets into his smoking gun.

'I want ya to run to that boulder and climb around it until ya on the slope again,' Hickok said firmly. 'Make the critter think you've had enough and are heading on back down the slope to our horses.'

Dix grabbed hold of Hickok's arm. 'And what are you gonna be doing while we do that, James Butler?'

Hickok leaned over and looked into the gun-fighter's eyes.

'I'm gonna kill the Phantom, Dixie.'

'How?'

'The Phantom knows he hit one of us, Dixie,' Hickok said. 'Ya gave out a mighty fine yelp when that bullet of his winged ya. I figure he don't know how good or bad his shot really was. For all he knows he's done for one of us. So when two of us run to the boulder he'll be curious.'

Dixie shook his head. 'How ya figure on killing him?'

Hickok reached down, plucked both his spurs from his boots and pushed them into Dix's pocket. 'Simple. I'm gonna move back through this cave nice and quiet, Dixie. When I see that white-skinned killer I intend killing him permanently.'

Dan and Dix looked at one another. Even the murky light inside the cave mouth could not hide their shared concern. It was Dan who decided to nod first.

'Do ya figure we gotta make us a real show of running away, Bill?' Dan asked as he checked his .45.

'Yep,' Hickok said. 'I want ya to make a real big noisy show of running away. Fire them hoglegs into every one of them cave entrances as ya go. Make that stinking sidewinder think he's won. He's loco but he's also used to winning. Seeing folks running scared away from his guns ain't nothing new to him.'

Dix licked his dry lips. 'I sure hope we don't make a mistake when we clamber around that boulder. It sure is a long fall down to the prairie from up here.'

'Count to ten and then run.' Hickok removed his hat and tossed it down on to the wet ground. His eyes narrowed and he walked into the darkness of the cave with one of his weapons jutting at hip level.

'Go,' Dix said after he had counted silently up to ten.

Both men ran towards the boulder, fanning the hammers of their guns at the series of black holes in the mountainside as they went.

Dix reached the boulder first. He dropped on to his belly as Dan moved to the side of the massive rock and looked over the rim of the ledge at the deadly drop. The precariousness of their situation became only too apparent. Dix threw himself down next to Dan and blasted at the countless shadows. Amid flashes of blinding light a massive earth-shaking thunderclap boomed out from inside the soup of swirling clouds above the rocky spires.

'There ain't no way we can get down under this boulder, Dixie,' Dan said as they both shook the spent cases from their guns and reloaded.

Dixie glanced at his friend. 'How come?'

'It's a sheer drop over the lip of the ledge,' Dan told him. He snapped his gun shut again and cocked its hammer. 'Ain't nothing but air to stand on.'

Then they saw him.

The Phantom emerged from another of the cave mouths with his guns held in his hands. This time he did not stop, fire and then retreat. This time he was coming in for the kill.

'Holy cow,' Dan croaked as he saw the hideous creature move ever closer. 'He's even uglier than

151

you and Bill said he was.'

Dix raised his gun and went to cock its hammer when the Phantom pulled on the trigger of the gun in his left hand. A red-hot taper hurtled from its already smoking barrel and hit the gun held aloft in Dix's hand. Dix winced as the .45 was torn from his gloved hand.

'Damn it all,' Dix cursed shaking his hand and checking his fingers. 'That critter ain't human. Nobody can shoot that fast and that accurate, Dan.'

Dan licked his lips and tried to sink into the sodden ground as he closed one eye and aimed. His finger stoked the trigger and fired.

The tail of the long trail coat was kicked up into the air as the Phantom kept heading at them.

'Either of ya know a backshooter named Hickok?' The voice of the Phantom bellowed out above the sound of the rumbling thunder.

The blood in the veins of both the veterans seemed to go icy cold as they heard the question uttered by the infamous white-skinned man who kept on walking towards them.

'Do ya?' the Phantom screamed out at the two men. 'I intend killing him. I intend killing the low-life who killed my pa.'

Dix grabbed the gun from Dan's hand, cocked it, then went to fire. Before his thumb had time to pull back on its hammer two shots homed in on him. One hit the gun and the other took the hat off his head. A trail of blood rolled down the wrinkled features of the stunned gunfighter from a gash on the crown of his head.

'Damn it all. He's playing with us,' Dix blurted out.

'I'd quit trying to kill him if I was you, Dixie. He's faster than you ever were,' Dan said. 'We're done for, boy.'

Dix screwed up his eyes against the rain and pushed himself up off the wet sand. 'I know Wild Bill Hickok, mister.'

'Ya know him?' The Phantom stopped. A flash of lightning lit up both men for the briefest of moments as they faced one another. Dix still had one of his guns sitting in its holster but wondered if there was even the slightest of chances that he might be able to use it before the Phantom fired again.

'I sure do know Hickok.' Dix nodded as rain washed more and more blood from the gash on his head down into his already burning eyes. 'A real bad critter and no mistake. Backshooter by all accounts.'

'Yeah. A backshooter.' The Phantom repeated the words and kept both his smoking guns aimed straight at the wounded gunfighter. 'Where is he? Do ya know where I can find him? I gotta kill him for what he done to my pa.'

'Was your pa the great Axil Gunn?' Dix asked.

The Phantom slowly nodded. His long white beard moved in the stiff breeze that cut across the mountain top between the peaks and spires.

'Yep. The great Axil Gunn.' The Phantom again repeated Dix's words. 'I have to avenge his murder, ya see? I have to find Hickok. Do ya know where Hickok is?'

'I'm right here.' Hickok walked out of the shadows of a cave mouth with both his guns held at belly height, aimed towards the strange, frightening figure. 'I'm Wild Bill Hickok.'

The Phantom swung on his boots, saw Hickok standing in the mouth of one of the caves and stared in disbelief. He went to raise his guns when Hickok squeezed both his triggers at the same moment. A mere heartbeat later he fired again.

As a flash of lightning lit up the entire top of the mountain the white-skinned man with the long beard suddenly had colour. The colour was red and it was spreading across his wet clothes from the four bullet holes in his body.

'Hickok?' the Phantom mumbled.

Hickok clawed his hammers back again and then sent two deadly accurate shots into the man's head. They shattered the skull and sent the Phantom staggering backwards. Only the edge of the ridge stopped the dead man from falling down into the prairie. The body lay on the very lip of the high precipice as blood spread from each of the bullet holes in his dead body.

Dix and Dan were first to reach the Phantom. They stared at the lifeless creature as Hickok moved slowly towards them.

'Reckon ya killed him,' Dan said.

Hickok pushed both his guns into their holsters and kicked angrily at the boots of his dead foe. The body went over the ledge and bounced like a rag doll as it crashed over the rough surface of the slope until it came to a sudden halt as it reached the level ground of the prairie.

'Ya feel any better for doing that, James Butler?' Dix asked his tall friend.

Hickok inhaled deeply. 'Nope. For some reason I don't feel any better at all, Dixie.'

'Leastways it's over, Bill,' Dan stated. 'Ya killed the Phantom.'

'Yep. I killed him OK. Twice by my reckoning, Danny boy.'

One by one the three men slowly began the descent into the darkness down to where they had left their horses.

FINALE

The brutal storm had at last passed over the jagged peaks of the mountains and mesas, leaving the scarred rocky pinnacles, like the trio of intrepid horsemen, to lick their wounds. A new day was soon to arrive and the stars and moon had given way to a glowing sky that stretched from horizon to horizon. Soon the sun would rise and start its daily ritual of baking the land known as Apache Springs dry. Far below the the high bloodstained ledge where Hickok, Dix and Dan had battled for their very lives there was an eerie silence. The brave men who had fought against the strange white-skinned man they knew as the Phantom could be seen steering their horses back towards the far-off way station. The only trophies they were taking back with them were the scars of their perilous ordeal.

The broken body of Axil Gunn's son remained at the foot of the steep cliff. Soon the coyotes and the vultures would come to feast upon its flesh and bone. Within days there would be nothing remaining of the man who had called himself the Phantom.

Soon only horrific memories would haunt the three men as they went on their way across the West. Memories of how close they had come to defeat. How close they had come to being the victims and not the victors in their encounter with a madman.

For the three horsemen it seemed to be over. Finally over. Somehow they had managed to destroy a monstrous creature and prevent him from killing even more innocent souls as he rode through the shadows of night in search of fresh prey.

But it was not over.

Not by a long shot.

As the sun crept up over the distant mountain range and its light sped across the prairie towards the high mesas, two figures emerged from one of the many caves on the lofty gore-splattered ledge. Two utterly different creatures who were somehow mother and son.

The tall albino man was identical to his dead brother who lay at the foot of the steep cliff. Devoid of any colour. Long white hair and beard and wearing identical black-lensed glasses to protect his sensitive eyes he remained as he had done after

157

escaping from the mental asylum back at Badwater. His name was Enio Gunn. He was the eldest of Axil Gunn's two sons.

The other creature was a small Cree woman who was less than five feet in height. Yet somehow her sons had always obeyed her every word, as though they were sacred texts and not the ravings of a twisted, sick mind. Long before, she had controlled their father Axil Gunn in the same fashion.

She was old now but no less evil. Her hair was grey with age and yet there was a mad insatiable fury still burning in her heartless soul, a madness which had infected those who had the misfortune of knowing her.

She led her wounded son to the very edge of the deadly ridge and looked down at the three riders who were getting further and further away from the mountains with every beat of her ancient heart.

'Look, my son,' she said bitterly, pointing into the distance with a bony finger. 'They ride as though they have triumphed. But they have not killed the Phantom. They have only killed his brother. You have been the true Phantom ever since your father was murdered by the man they called Hickok.'

Enio Gunn said nothing. He stood beside his mother like all obedient sons do when in the presence of their overbearing parents. Enio Gunn was the mirror image of his dead father and brother. He touched his sleeve and then looked at the blood upon his pale fingertips.

'I'm wounded, Ma,' the Phantom said. 'Wounded when I helped brother Axil fighting those evil men.'

'You drew their fire from your brother,' she said. 'But it was not enough to save him. He was only ever a shadow of you. You are like your father. A true avenger. The real Phantom.'

'My arm's busted,' Gunn quietly snarled. 'Hickok busted my arm with a lucky shot, Ma.'

She rested a comforting hand on her son's bleeding arm. 'For twenty years we awaited your return, Enio. Waited for you to reclaim your father's legacy. To avenge his murder by Hickok.'

The Phantom nodded.

'Hickok has made his last mistake, my son. When your wounds have healed the Phantom shall ride again. Shall kill again. Now you have another to avenge. Now you must avenge your brother's slaying.'

'I'll kill a thousand worthless critters more to get Hickok in my gun sights again, Ma,' Gunn vowed. 'He don't know it yet but he's gonna pay. Pay with his life.'

'Good. Now come with me before the sun burns your skin.' The Cree woman turned and walked back into the nearest cave entrance with her son in her wake. 'I shall heal your wounds. Shall make you stronger than you have ever been before, Enio.'

Unknown to Hickok as he and his pals rode on to the way station, it was still not over.

The Phantom still lived.

Home Library Service (For Staff Use Only)

1	2	3	4	5	6	7	8	9
		326A						
								27094